GRAVE DOUBTS

GRAVE DOUBTS

by John Peel

Cover illustration by Stephen Brennan
Illustrated by Eric Shawn Cherry

Publishers • Grosset & Dunlap • New York

For my sister, Elizabeth,
of whom I have only good memories,
and for Martin—J.P.

Text copyright © 1993 by John Peel. Cover illustration copyright © 1993 by Stephen Brennan. Interior illustrations copyright © 1993 by Eric Shawn Cherry. Published by Grosset & Dunlap, Inc., which is a member of The Putnam & Grosset Group, New York. SHOCKERS is a trademark belonging to The Putnam & Grosset Group. Published simultaneously in Canada. Printed in the U.S.A. Library of Congress Catalog Card Number: 92-72821 ISBN 0-448-40528-8 A B C D E F G H I J

Contents

1

Bad Memories

"What's going on?"

Matt Howard stared, puzzled, from his bedroom window down over the fence that separated the Howard house from the old house next door. The place had been closed for years. The paint was flaking, the siding was warped, and one of the windows had been broken by a stray baseball earlier in the summer. But now the front door was open, and two men were moving some furniture into the house.

His mother, who had just brought up his clean laundry, followed his gaze. "Oh. It's true, then."

"What is?" asked Matt.

"Uncle Joey's coming home." His mother frowned slightly. "Do you remember Uncle Joey?"

Matt shook his head. "I didn't know I *had* an Uncle Joey."

"Well, you don't, really. His name is Mr. Ciprelli, but you always called him Uncle Joey when you were a lot younger. You really liked him, until—" She broke off and tried to cover her nervousness by handing him his shirts. "Do you remember anything about him?"

He tried, but the name didn't ring any bells. "Nope."

"Well, he's been . . . away for about ten years," his mother added. "I guess you've forgotten all about him by now." From the expression on her face, Matt could tell that she was *hoping* he'd forgotten about Uncle Joey. That was odd.

"Where's he been?" Matt asked, watching

the men move the furniture into the old house. "And how come he's moved back?"

Mrs. Howard paused, obviously reluctant to discuss the issue. But she also knew she couldn't just remain silent. "Well," she said with a sigh, "he's been in a hospital. A *mental* hospital. He must have just been discharged."

"Oh. Is he nuts?"

"Matthew!" His mother was shocked. "If they've let him out, then he must be cured. And I don't ever want you to use words like that when he might hear you!"

"Sorry," he said, without really meaning it. "Then he must have been nu—*crazy* at one time."

"Yes. He was." His mother chewed her bottom lip and then decided to plunge on. "He loved your sister dearly. And when she was killed, he claimed to have seen . . . things. He harassed the police with his silly ideas, and eventually he was sent to a hospital." She glanced at him sharply. "You don't remember any of that?"

"Not a thing." Matt concentrated. He could remember his sister, Penny, of course. And a little bit about her being killed. But he didn't remember anything about this mysterious Uncle Joey. "Well, if he's okay now, I guess there's no problem."

Mrs. Howard looked out of the window. She didn't seem relieved. "I hope not."

Matt walked outside and watched the men finish their work. He was puzzled about this Uncle Joey character and wanted to see what the man was like. The movers ignored him, concentrating on their job instead. Bored, Matt wandered off. He didn't pay any attention to the old house until a car drove up.

On the side was a sign with the words: BROOKVILLE HOSPITAL. The driver stayed in the car, but two men got out of the back seat. One was obviously a doctor. He wore a white coat and fussed over the older man. That one had to be Uncle Joey.

Matt watched him carefully. He didn't *look* crazy. Just like an old man—thinning gray-white hair, a wrinkled face, a slight stoop when he walked. Then he glanced up and saw Matt looking at him. Matt started to wave at the man, but his arm stopped in mid-air. Uncle Joey's face twisted in anger when he saw Matt, then—almost instantly—went blank again. The old man looked at the doctor, who hadn't seen the angry expression.

But Matt had. And, what was worse, Matt *did* remember the man's face from somewhere in a long-closed part of his memory. And the sight that had triggered the memory was Uncle Joey's face twisted in anger. . . .

Why?

The two men hurried into the old house. Matt, shaken by the strange memory, went into his own house to get something to drink. What had that all been about? Matt poured himself a glass of milk. Uncle Joey clearly remembered Matt, even though he'd changed a lot in the last ten years. He could only have been about four when Uncle Joey went to the hospital. So why was the guy still angry?

Matt sat shaking in his bed, clutching the blanket in his hands as if he were a child again, and not fourteen years old. He knew it was silly, but he couldn't force his fingers apart to drop the blanket. Sweat trickled down both his face and back, and the memories of the nightmare that had awakened him kept playing over and over in his tormented mind. The fact that it was now light outside didn't relieve his terror at all.

*   *   *

Matt is young in the dream, maybe four years old. He sees a ball roll through the basement door in the kitchen of his house. It bounces down the stairs, bump, bump on each step. Matt knows he has to follow the ball, but he doesn't want to. The basement is dark, full of deep shadows and unknown horrors. A single light bulb hangs from the ceiling and casts eerie shadows. He goes down the stairs, bump, bump, like the ball he is following. The steps are so steep, much too big for his four-year-old legs. He has to get the ball. But there is something else down here, something else he has to see.

Something evil.

Nothing makes sense in the dream. His mind flashes from one horrible scene to another. Now, he is in the basement, but he is crouching in a dusty corner. He has no choice. There is something dangerous down here with him, and he has to hide from it in the shadows.

From the corner he sees his sister, Penny. She is so beautiful, a radiant, pure light in the gloomy darkness. Her long blond hair falls straight to her shoulders. Her bright blue eyes are set in a pale, pretty face. And she is so neatly dressed, with no dirt or wrinkles on her clothes from playing. His sister's face is sweet, gentle, and innocent.

Then comes the blood.

A flood of it washes over him—warm, sticky, with a stench that makes his stomach churn. How can so much blood come from one person?

He stares down at Penny on the floor. A huge knife is sticking out of her. He bends down and touches her, but she won't get up. He whispers her name, "Penny, Penny." Maybe she is pretending, maybe she will get up.

But Penny is not pretending. She is dead, and Matt does not want her to be.

*   *   *

What a terrible nightmare. Matt had never had this dream before, yet everything in it seemed strangely familiar. His parents had told him a little bit about Penny's murder. *He* didn't remember anything himself. He had only been four years old at the time, and had locked away all memories of the event.

Matt hardly remembered *anything* about his big sister. He knew she was as beautiful as the vision in his nightmare because of the family photo album. It was full of pictures of Penny that his mother treasured. "My darling, my angel," his mother would say softly when she looked at the book.

He had loved Penny. She'd been eleven when she died, seven years older than Matt. He'd looked up to his big sister and adored her.

Well, he thought he did. He could remember that she was always so sweet and gentle. She never raised her voice and never got mad. She used to put her arms around him, protecting him. But there was something else in his mind that wouldn't come out, something that made him feel uneasy about his sister. Was it because she was always so sweet, and he had always been a little monster?

His mom often talked about Penny. "Such a gentle child," she always said. "She would never get into fights with other children. Not at all like you."

That part was certainly true. He did get into

fights somehow, ever since he was little. His temper seemed to have a very short fuse. He had few friends at school, because sooner or later he always fought with them. Penny, he knew, had been really popular and had lots of friends.

Matt couldn't shake the idea that this was more than just a nightmare. It almost seemed like déjà vu, as if he had seen it happen before. Then a new idea occurred to him. Maybe he really *had* seen all this happen before. Maybe this entire nightmare was based on his *memories* of the murder—memories that his four-year-old mind had locked away, but were now breaking free. Matt had been told by his parents that he'd found his sister's body. But now he wondered if he had really been downstairs the whole time. Could he have been hiding while his sister was murdered? Could he have seen everything?

What a strange idea. Matt could hardly believe that he would *forget* his sister's murder. He tried desperately to remember something, *anything*, about that horrible day. What was real and what was only nightmare? If he had been in the basement when Penny was murdered, wouldn't his parents have told him so? Matt didn't want to believe that he'd seen Penny get killed, but why else would that dream seem so real?

He was no longer shivering in terror. His heartbeat had finally slowed down to nearly normal. Matt dragged himself out of bed, completely drained. He parted the curtain at his window to see what the weather was like. It was grey outside. The sun was just coming up.

Next door, Uncle Joey was sitting on his front porch. It almost looked as though he were watching Matt's room.

Matt quickly closed his curtains, definitely spooked. This was *really* weird. All Uncle Joey ever seemed to do since he moved back home a week ago was sit on the porch or stand by his window and look at the Howard house.

No, Matt thought, look at *me*.

He shook his head to drive out the crazy notion. There was no reason why Uncle Joey would be watching him. He was just some lonely old guy with nothing better to do all day than shuffle around in his threadbare sweaters and old slippers and watch what was going on outside.

Maybe he liked looking at the house because it reminded him of Penny. Hadn't Mom told him that Uncle Joey loved Penny? *I guess everyone did*, Matt thought.

Or maybe there was another reason. All week, Matt had gotten the feeling that there was something still wrong with Uncle Joey. It wasn't just the old clothes, or that Uncle Joey never seemed to go anywhere. It was more than that. The doctors said that he was better, but Matt didn't buy it. Uncle Joey tried to look normal whenever people were around, but sometimes Matt saw him sitting on his porch with a grim expression on his face. His eyes would flash with anger, and he would mutter something to himself. Matt had begun to wonder if Uncle Joey was dangerous, or had been in the past.

Could Uncle Joey have been the murderer?

Matt admitted to himself that he was really jumping to conclusions. The idea that Uncle Joey could be a murderer was pretty far-fetched. Just because the man was strange didn't mean he was a homicidal maniac. Matt didn't think the police had ever accused him of murder, and Mom and Dad had never said they thought Uncle Joey had anything to do with Penny's death. They treated him carefully, but nothing more. They had been pretty friendly with him all week. Mom had even cooked an extra dinner for him a couple of times and taken it to his house.

But Matt couldn't get rid of the memory of Uncle Joey's face, twisted in anger. Matt didn't understand why Uncle Joey seemed to hate him so much, or why he would want to spend all his time watching the Howard house. People didn't act that way unless they had a reason.

Maybe Uncle Joey knew more about what happened the day of the murder than Matt could remember. It seemed more and more to Matt that his nightmare was not just a bad dream. Maybe Matt really had been hiding in the basement when Penny was killed, and now he was starting to remember the whole thing. If he'd seen it, and if Uncle Joey was the murderer, he would want to keep an eye on Matt—after all, Matt could have been the only witness.

Matt wished his dream had given him more clues about what had happened that day. As it was, it scared the daylights out of him and didn't really help. This was all so strange. First Uncle Joey returning, and now this nightmare.

Though it was barely six o'clock in the morning, Matt knew he was awake for good. For one thing, he was too afraid of having the nightmare again to get back in bed and go to sleep. As he started putting his clothes on, he tried to think of other things, but images of his nightmare kept haunting him.

He *had* been in the basement the day that Penny had been killed. He was sure of that. He had discovered her body, his parents had told him. Or more likely, he had been downstairs the whole time. Either way, there was a good chance he'd seen the killer, whether it was Uncle Joey or someone else. But had he been so terrified that he'd blocked out all details of the killing for ten years? Were those memories coming back to the surface now? Would he soon remember who had killed his sister?

And if the nightmares *were* memories, and he *did* remember who had killed Penny—then what? Could he go to the police? Would they listen to him? Would they believe him? Or would they think he was just a crazy kid with an overactive imagination?

Was he just a crazy kid with an overactive imagination?

He went downstairs to the kitchen and poured himself some juice. As he closed the refrigerator door, he glanced at the calendar on it. It was one of those freebies from the Humane Society, with kittens on it that were cute enough to make you gag on your breakfast.

From the calendar, Matt realized that it was ten years ago this month that Penny had died.

That's why Mom had been so weird lately. She always broke down around this time of year. Matt couldn't blame her, really, but after ten years you'd think she could have learned to accept things. He knew she never would, though. Unless . . . If the killer was ever found and jailed, maybe then Mom would be able to get on with things.

As it was, she spent a lot of time brooding over the photo album and telling him what a saint Penny had been, and how she must be in heaven now, looking down on them with love in her heart for them all. And that she'd been taken from them by some depraved maniac who had undoubtedly killed God-knew-how-many other kids because the police hadn't been able to catch him.

Matt couldn't stand it when his mom acted that way. Always saying Penny this, Penny that, and how awful life was now that she was gone.

Then Matt felt guilty. After all, Penny had been his only sister. She had looked after him for four years, and if she'd lived, she'd have looked after him for fourteen. Didn't he owe her something for that? How could he be thinking only of himself right now?

He had a few dollars left over from his birthday a couple of weeks earlier. Probably enough to buy a small bunch of flowers. The cemetery, where Penny's grave was, was only a fifteen-minute bike ride away. Who knew—maybe it would please Mom if he left some flowers on his sister's grave. It would make *him* feel better, anyway.

2

A Trip to the Cemetery

Matt got off his bike at the cemetery entrance. The bunch of flowers he'd bought hadn't suffered from being carried in his backpack. They were mostly white carnations, which looked nice. He'd almost turned green when he'd seen the blood red ones in the shop. They reminded him of the pool of Penny's blood from his nightmare. Thankfully, the girl in the shop hadn't suggested any of those. She had insisted on adding the white stuff she called baby's breath and a handful of bright green ferns to the bunch, and then wrapped them in paper. As he clutched the flowers, Matt felt a little embarrassed.

He hadn't told his mom where he was going, and she'd been too depressed to ask. As he'd ridden off from his house, Matt wondered if Uncle Joey was watching him from his window. Did he know where Matt had gone? Was he planning on following him?

Stop it! he told himself. He was getting spooked by the crazy old man, that was all. Why would Uncle Joey want to follow him?

Leaving his bike chained at the entrance, Matt set off down the pathway toward his sister's grave. He knew that some people hated cemeteries and wouldn't go near them. Matt had never felt that way. He felt a real sense of peace here. He'd read a poem in English class once by some old guy named Andrew Marvell. Most of it he'd forgotten, but one line stuck in his mind: "The grave's a fine and private place." He liked the sound of it. It made death sound as though it were peaceful and quiet, just like this graveyard. He felt relaxed here.

He wasn't the only one there. An old lady

was on a bench, throwing bread crumbs to a flock of hungry sparrows that hopped and pecked all around her. *They* weren't afraid of this place. Only people were scared of graveyards. That was silly. There was nothing frightening here.

He heard the sound of cars turning into the entrance and paused to watch. A hearse—long, black, and shiny—led a procession of cars into the grounds. Matt had always liked the look of hearses—kind of like the limos that rock stars rode around in. For most people, hearses were the only limos they'd ever ride in. Rich or poor, it didn't matter—they all ended up here, in their own fine and private places. One day he'd come to the cemetery and never leave.

Ugh. Enough depressing talk. As he walked, Matt thought about the arriving funeral. People would be crying and grim, he knew. Some would be feeling sorry for themselves, or for the people the dead person left behind. Some would be feeling sorry for the person who'd died. Others would just want to get out of there and go somewhere more "fun." The only person who'd be feeling okay would be

the one who was being buried.

He arrived at the grave. It was nothing fancy. His dad had refused to buy the big marble angel Mom had wanted. Matt knew his dad had felt it was a waste of money, spending it on the dead. Mom hadn't spoken to Dad for weeks afterward, but the small headstone was much better. Some of the monuments in the graveyard were *tacky*. Huge open Bibles (how many of the dead had opened a real Bible when they were alive?), or those giant angels. Six-foot-tall crosses, some even carved with the faces of the dead people on them. The mausoleums—houses for the dead—weren't so bad if you liked your family so much you wanted to share a room with them after you died. Matt thought he would rather be in his *own* grave.

Penelope Anne Howard, the small marble stone read. And, underneath, *1971–1983. Beloved daughter and sister*. Simple, but direct. At the foot of the neat grave was a small bowl for flowers. There were some recent ones still in it, but they were beginning to curl at the tips and turn brown. Placing his flowers on the grave for a moment, Matt pulled out the old flowers and threw them in the closest trash can. Then he carefully arranged the fresh flowers in the bowl.

As he worked, he thought about Penny. He wished he'd had the chance to know her better. Everyone always told him what a nice girl she'd been, and how the two of them were inseparable. All he could remember was her smiling face. But he wished he knew why at the same time he had uneasy feelings about her.

It had to be because people constantly compared him to his older sister. She must have been perfect. Everyone seemed to think so, and there was no way he could compete with perfection. Matt didn't understand how someone could be so *good* all the time. What was she, a saint or something?

Matt knew *he* was no saint. He never *meant* to get into trouble, but that's exactly what happened. It was like trouble followed him around, wherever he went. *And so did Penny's perfect reputation*, Matt thought. He couldn't shake the comparisons, at home or at school. If he had a dollar for every time someone had said to him, "Why can't you be good like Penny was?", he'd be rich by now.

Ever since he could remember, school teachers had thrown Penny in his face whenever he'd done something wrong. He'd gone to the same elementary school that she'd attended, and *everyone* had a story to tell about "sweet Penny." Although he was young at the time, Matt couldn't forget those stories, no matter how hard he tried.

His second grade teacher, Miss Norman, had been particularly fond of Penny. One day, he'd been goofing off in class with some other boys. They weren't doing anything really bad, just flying paper airplanes and throwing spitballs at some of the girls. Miss Norman told them to stop, just as his friend, Billy Peters, launched a spitball right at her.

"Matthew Howard, get up here this instant," she said to him in a firm voice.

"But . . . but, I . . . ," he stammered, trying to tell her that *he* hadn't done it.

"No buts about it, come up here *now*." Matt turned beet red and slowly walked to the front of the class. He had to stand there while Miss Norman told all the kids about "Matt's wonderful older sister, Penny, who is no longer with us." She said that Penny had been a good little girl, always neat and on time and very quiet unless she was answering a question in class. She would *never* be rude or throw spitballs, especially at a teacher.

At the end of her speech, Miss Norman had tears in her eyes. She looked at Matt and said, "How did you end up so bad when your sister was so good?"

Matt cringed at this memory as he knelt over Penny's grave. "All those teachers loved you so much and hated me," he whispered to her tombstone. He had finished arranging the flowers, and sat down next to the grave. Although memories like that one still hurt, they weren't as painful as what his mother had said only a few months ago.

Matt had gotten into a fight at school with Kenny Morris. He couldn't even remember now how it started. Anyway, they began punching each other in gym class. Pretty soon it was an all-out fist fight. Matt hit Kenny hard enough to give him a black eye, but Kenny also got in a few good punches before the gym teacher broke up the fight. Blood flowed from Matt's nose and his upper lip was swollen. He also thought he sprained his wrist, or at least jammed it.

Because it was Matt's third fight that semester, the principal called his mother and had her come in to talk about his "problem." Matt glumly sat outside the office, expecting the worst. His wrist ached and he could taste blood in his mouth. He was sure there would be no sympathy for him.

He was right. His mother stormed out of the principal's office, grabbed him by the arm and dragged him to the car. "You're suspended for a week from school and grounded for two months, Matthew," she said sternly as they got into the car. "I can't believe it. We keep telling you not to fight, but you just never listen."

Matt sullenly stared out the window as they drove out of the parking lot. His mother shook her head. "You're almost more trouble than you're worth. And poor Penny's the one who had to die!"

Mom had tried to make up for it later, but it didn't work. Even now, it hurt him. He knew everyone liked Penny better, but did they have to say so? He stroked the grass on top of Penny's grave. It was a little like a blanket.

What if he had been the one killed? What would it be like, he wondered, to be lying underground? Well, no teachers would be around to tell him what a good student Penny was. No parents would say what a great daughter she was. And there'd be no awful nightmares about the murder. It would be peaceful. That would be a good thing, he thought, about being dead.

There was a funny feeling at the back of his neck. The sort of thing he felt sometimes at the barber when they used the razor to trim the back of his hair. Prickly, a bit like an electric shock. He shuddered, then looked around. He felt as if somebody was watching him. . . .

For a second, he couldn't move. His heart seemed to pause, his blood to stop still in his veins.

Standing there, opposite him, was a young girl. She was on a slight rise in the ground, about thirty feet away. Behind her, the gravestones fell away down a gentle slope. She stood with her hands clasped in front of her, staring at him.

Her long blond hair was rustled by the

breeze, snaking out as if alive. Her clear blue eyes (how did he *know* they were blue at this distance?) were focused on him. Her plain white blouse and skirt were crisp and almost shone in the sunlight.

"Penny . . ." he whispered. It looked *exactly* like the sister of his few memories. He glanced down at the grave, as if expecting to see a door in the grass open to let her out. Then he looked back at the hill, and the figure was gone.

A ghost? Penny, almost ten years after her murder, back from the dead?

No! He didn't believe in ghosts! That was silly Halloween stuff. When you were dead, you were dead. Period. You didn't come back.

If you *did*, then Penny would have been back before this. He remembered in a rush how he'd hoped after her murder that she'd come back. She never had then, so why should she now?

No, Penny was dead, lying in the grave here. That girl might *look* like Penny, but it couldn't really be his sister. He jumped to his feet and ran to where the girl had been standing. There was no sign of her now. Had he imagined her? He looked at the grass and saw

the imprint of a shoe. *Someone* had stood here. Not a ghost, unless ghosts wore shoes! A real person.

He remembered the hearse and shook his head. He was so stupid—the girl was probably one of the people at that funeral. She'd just spotted him and—

Then he saw the grave site where the funeral was taking place. It was beyond Penny's grave, much deeper into the cemetery. He frowned. If the girl had come from that funeral, she'd have to pass him to stand where he'd seen her. And he was certain nobody had passed by him.

Weird . . .

In any event, where had she gone? She wasn't standing here now, and she hadn't walked toward the burial now taking place. There was no sign of anyone but the old woman feeding the sparrows, and the people at the funeral.

Matt felt very uneasy. Okay, maybe she was hiding—there were plenty of large headstones she could duck down behind. But *why* would she do that? Nothing came to mind. And if she wasn't hiding from him, then the only other explanation was that she was a ghost. *That* was impossible. Wasn't it?

He walked back to Penny's grave, looking over his shoulder several times as he did so. There was no further sign of the odd girl. He wished that made him feel better, but it didn't. He frowned as he came to a halt by the grave. On the grass lay a blue envelope. Puzzled, he picked it up. There was nothing written on it, and it wasn't sealed. Puzzled, he opened the flap. There were two sheets of paper inside. He unfolded the first and stared at it in disbelief.

It was a photocopy of an article from the local newspaper, dated ten years ago this month. The story was about the murder of Penny Howard and had a picture of her smiling. Penny's face looked a lot like the girl he'd just seen.

The second piece of paper was a letter. He jammed it into his back pocket. He felt cold all of a sudden. What could this mean? Who had left the envelope for him? Surely not the girl— she'd disappeared. Somebody must have put the envelope on the grave while he had gone looking for her. But who—and why? Slowly, thoughtfully, he cleared up the paper that his flowers had been wrapped in and then looked down at his sister's final resting place one last time.

He hoped she *was* resting . . . and not out walking.

Stop that! he ordered himself. This was no way to treat matters. He was simply spooked by everything that had happened lately. That was all. He was making mountains out of molehills. Determined not to allow his emotions to rule him, he turned his back on Penny's grave and walked back to where he had left his bike.

By the time Matt reached home, he was convinced that this was simply some sick joke. Maybe one of the boys he'd beaten up was playing an elaborate gag on him to get revenge. No, he decided. No one he knew had the brains to do anything so clever. If it *was* a trick, it was being played by someone smart. And someone who knew where he'd gone.

Uncle Joey?

Matt stared at his neighbor's house as he took his bike into the garage. He wondered if the old man was staring out the window now, watching his every move. Who knew what was going on in his crazy old mind?

Forget it! Matt said to himself fiercely. He's just a lonely old man. Refusing to give in to his panic, Matt stormed out of the garage. He was about to enter the house when he realized that he hadn't checked the day's mail. It was one of his jobs—as a kid he had always enjoyed running to the mailbox as soon as the mailman came by. His parents had let him get the mail and bring it in, thinking it was cute. Over the years the thrill had gone, but the task remained.

Opening the box, he took out a handful of letters and a couple of those stupid free newspapers that were mostly ads for local businesses. Out of habit, he flipped through the letters. Junk mail, mostly, and the cable TV bill.

It reminded him of the letter in his back pocket. Instead of going in the front door, he walked around the back of the house and into the kitchen. He put the mail on the kitchen table, then shot up the stairs to his room.

Closing the door, he kicked off his sneakers. Then he dragged out his odd letter.

He began to read. It was another photocopy, but this time it wasn't from any newspaper. It was a poem that seemed kind of familiar, though he couldn't remember where he had seen it.

Because I could not stop for Death—
He kindly stopped for me—
The Carriage held but just Ourselves—
and Immortality.

We slowly drove—He knew no haste
And I had put away
My labor and my leisure too,
For His Civility—

We passed the School, where Children strove
At Recess—in the Ring—
We passed the Fields of Gazing Grain—
We passed the Setting Sun—

Or rather—He passed Us—
The Dews drew quivering and chill—
For only Gossamer, my Gown—
My Tippet—only Tulle—

We paused before a House that seemed
A Swelling of the Ground—
The Roof was scarcely visible—
The Cornice—in the Ground—

Since then—'tis Centuries—and yet
Feels shorter than the Day
I first surmised the Horses' Heads
Were toward Eternity—

What a weird poem, with all those dashes and strange words. Matt stared at the poem again. Who was that lady poet, the one who had written all those poems about death. . . . Suddenly Matt remembered. Emily Dickinson! He had to read some of her poems for English class last semester, and hated every minute of it. He came home from school one day whining about how he couldn't understand anything she wrote. Mom had been in the kitchen making dinner.

"Why do we have to read these stupid poems?" he complained to her. "I'm not learning anything, and this woman is really depressing! She writes about graves and snakes and flies and—" Matt stopped short. His mother was giving him a funny look.

"Emily Dickinson was your sister's favorite poet," Mom said quietly. "Penny loved everything she wrote."

Matt remembered how he had shut up after that. No more complaining about Emily Dickinson. But why would anyone leave the poem on Penny's grave for him to find?

Matt saw something handwritten at the bottom of the page. Maybe this would be the answer. But all it said was:

I remember. Do you?

Remember what? Matt was *really* confused now. This was getting to be more than a joke. Why Penny's favorite poet, and the creepy poem about death? And what did the last handwritten line mean?

Suddenly angry, he ran downstairs. Maybe Mom might be able to tell him. After all, she knew more about Penny than he did! But as he entered the living room, he saw that his mother had fallen asleep while looking at Penny's scrapbook. She was sleeping quietly in her favorite chair. The scrapbook with all its memories of Penny lay on the floor by the chair. As he went to pick it up, Matt saw it was open to a birthday card Penny had sent Mom. In her big, bold handwriting, it said: *I'll always remember what you've done for me, Mom.*

Matt's heart nearly stopped. A chill seemed to close around him.

The word *remember* made it unmistakable. The handwriting on the birthday card was identical to that on the note from the grave.

The poem and its message were from *Penny*.

3

Penny for Your Thoughts?

That night, Matt lay in bed for ages, twisting, turning, unable to sleep—and scared of what would happen when he did doze off. The events of the day kept hammering on his mind, demanding attention. He refused to think about them, afraid of what he might discover. All he wanted was peace. Was that too much to ask?

Eventually, he slept. But not peacefully. The nightmare returned, just as terrifying as the night before. It was as if something were trying

to break out of his memories, something pow-
erful and strong but still hidden from view.

*   *   *

*He is four years old again and playing in the
kitchen. His ball rolls through the door into the
basement and bounces down the stairs. Matt can't
remember why, but it is very important that he goes
downstairs after the ball. Someone is in trouble; that
is all he knows.*

*But the basement is dark and scary. All he can
see are terrible, deep shadows. He walks slowly down
the stairs. He sees a single light bulb gently swing
from the ceiling.*

*Everything happens so quickly. There is anger
and pain, a voice shouting loudly, and then Matt is
crouching in a dark corner. Penny looms before him,
sweet and innocent in the light. But Matt can't
move or talk—he has to be absolutely still in his
hiding place. He must hide from someone, someone
who can hurt him.*

*And then comes the blood, flooding the basement
floor. Penny lies in a pool of it with the knife sticking
out of her. "Penny, Penny," Matt whispers. She
has to wake up! She has to stop playing!*

This time, Matt knows he and Penny aren't alone

in the basement. There is someone else with them, someone who has an angry face that Matt can't quite recognize. Someone who looks a lot like . . .

Uncle Joey!

*   *   *

Matt screamed and woke up, his heart pounding wildly. He breathed deeply, trying to calm his feverish thoughts. What did this mean? Was it proof that Uncle Joey was the murderer? Or did his face just pop into the dream because Matt thought he *could* have killed Penny?

As he sat, shivering in the early-morning light, he wondered what he wanted. Which would be better: finally to see the horror that caused his nightmares, or to bury it forever? Did he have a choice?

There was no point in trying to get back to sleep again. He felt tired out, but he was too afraid of his dreams to sleep. What he badly needed was a long, dreamless rest. He knew he wouldn't get it.

Throwing on some old clothes, he walked over to the window and parted the curtain.

Sure enough, Uncle Joey was standing at his front door, looking over at the Howard house. Matt wearily closed his curtains. Didn't the guy ever sleep? Didn't he do anything with his life but stare at Matt's house? Why was he doing this? Matt wished he had the courage to confront the old man and ask him directly. But who knew what would happen if he tried that? Uncle Joey was probably just waiting for a chance to get Matt alone—for what? Was he the person who'd killed Penny? And if not, why was he in Matt's dream?

Going downstairs, Matt made himself some breakfast. He didn't really feel hungry, but he needed some food in his stomach. It was just mechanical—crunch whatever he had just poured out of the cereal box, swallow the milk. He glanced at the clock. Not even eight yet. Dad would be up soon and off to work. Matt didn't want to be around for that. Over the past ten years, his father had sunk himself completely into his work, as if afraid to become as close to another person as he had been to Penny. His dad had adored her—half the pictures in the scrapbooks of Penny had him in

them. She'd been a bit of a tomboy at times, and she was crazy about sports. His father had loved that.

Since her death, he'd never even tossed a ball for Matt to catch. And he'd been—well, not exactly cold, but never very warm. As if he were always afraid that Matt would die soon, and didn't want to get too attached to him. For Matt, it had been kind of like growing up with a zombie—always there, but never really alive.

It was best not to get in his way while he got ready for work. Luckily, Matt had somewhere to go this morning. Once a week, he attended a summer school class in math at his junior high school. He had flunked the class during the school year because he wasn't that good in math and he had hated the teacher. Mrs. Perry was his teacher now. She wasn't so bad, and Matt thought he would actually pass the class this time.

I can't believe I'm looking forward to going to school, he thought as he grabbed his backpack and walked outside. But he needed to get away from the house for awhile, and although math wasn't exactly *fun*, at least it would keep him from thinking about the nightmares.

Matt threw his backpack over his shoulder and wheeled his bike out of the garage. As he walked his bike down to the street, he thought about the picture of Uncle Joey that had popped into his dream last night. Those hate-filled eyes, the mouth opened wide in horror . . . what did this all mean? Suddenly, a tall, thin, stooped figure stepped out in front of him from behind a tree.

It was Uncle Joey. And he had that same hateful gleam in his eyes.

Matt started to panic. He wanted to jump on his bike and get away as fast as he could, away from that twisted face. But instead, he exploded in a fit of anger. He threw his bike down on the ground and yelled, "I'm fed up with you always watching my house. What do you want?" Now let the old man try to deny that he had been spying on Matt!

Instead, Uncle Joey bent down, narrowed his eyes, and looked Matt right in the face. "Ralph. Remember Ralph?" he said quietly. He then walked into his own driveway. Uncle Joey paused on his front porch, gave Matt another angry look, and then walked inside. The slam of the door echoed in the still air.

Matt stared at the door, confused. What was that about? He didn't know anyone named Ralph. There was no one in his class by that name. It was not a very "in" name for guys these days. Kind of a joke name, really.

But somewhere, buried deep in his memories, the name *did* mean something. . . .

Well, there was no time to think about it. He was late for class. Matt picked his bike up, jumped on, and pedaled quickly to school. All the way there he tried to focus on today's lesson, but the equations he was supposed to learn got jumbled up in his head. As he rode into the school parking lot, the only thing he could hear was Uncle Joey's voice. "Remember Ralph? Remember Ralph? Remember . . ."

"Hey Howard, hurry up, you're going to be late!" Matt snapped out of his trance. That was Tom Myers on the school steps, a friend of his in the same class. Not exactly a friend, Matt thought darkly. More like one of the few boys he hadn't gotten into a fight with yet. Matt coasted up to the bike rack.

"Cool it, Myers, I'm coming," he yelled

back. Matt chained his bike and walked up the steps with Tom.

"Great, man," Tom said. "Now I won't be the only one late." Matt hardly heard what Tom said. As he walked into the building, he caught a glimpse of a girl with long blond hair standing to the side of the parking lot. She looked a little young for his class, but maybe she was in one of the lower grades at his school. Although he couldn't see her too well, Matt could tell she was wearing a white skirt and blouse and carrying a small purse.

And she was watching him.

When Matt paused in the doorway to look more closely at her, she turned and walked quickly away. "Weird," he whispered.

"Do you know that girl?" Tom asked him as they walked down the hall. "She sure looked like she knew *you*."

"Uh, no, I don't know any girls," Matt muttered. But he *did* know her, sort of. That *had* to be the girl he saw at the cemetery yesterday, the girl who looked like Penny. She had the same hair, the same clothes, the same focused look on her face. But what was she doing here?

He slowly walked down the hall, lost in

thought. Tom grabbed his arm and pulled him along. "Hurry up, Matt, Mrs. Perry's going to be steamed." When they walked into the classroom, she gave them a frosty look.

"You're late, boys," she said. "We're on page forty."

Matt sunk into his seat. This was too much for him. All he wanted was peace and quiet and an end to his nightmares. Now, he had even more questions about what was going on. Mrs. Perry's voice droned on endlessly. He had no idea where they were in the lesson, and he didn't even care. Matt vaguely heard the class laughing, and then finally heard his name called loudly.

"Matt Howard, I asked you a question," Mrs. Perry said sharply. "Weren't you listening to me?"

"I'm sorry, what did you say?" Matt asked weakly.

She spoke to him more kindly now. "Matt, you look sick. Why don't you go home today and take it easy."

He smiled at her gratefully as he got out of his seat, though there was no way he could take *anything* easy now. Not after this day.

Matt slowly walked through the empty halls and out to the parking lot. He kept thinking about the name Ralph. Who *was* Ralph?

Maybe he should ask Mom. She might know. A relative, or an old friend? Maybe someone who used to live in the neighborhood? After Penny's murder, several people had moved away from the street. It was as if they felt that the killing might spread. Or that the Howard house polluted the block. Or that one of *their* kids might be next. But there hadn't been any killings since Penny's death.

Even if it was the name of a kid who'd moved away, why had Uncle Joey mentioned it? Matt shook his head as he unchained his bike and started toward home.

It was all so confusing. He saw the article and poem on his dresser where he had put them yesterday after finding them on Penny's grave. He wanted to tear them up, to destroy them and go on with his life. But, instead, he put them in a box in his closet. It was the one in which he kept his old baseball cards. That collection had seemed so important to him a couple of years ago. He never looked at it now. Times and people change.

Was his whole life going to be like this? Matt had on and off felt a sense of doom, at least since Penny's death. Now he had fresh fears and new questions to worry about as well. He wished he had a really good friend to talk to, someone who would at least listen to him. He was friendly with Tom, but he just didn't think Tom would understand. There was no one else who would, either. He never seemed to get really close to *anyone*. Something inside of him made him act funny sometimes, and he got angry and struck out at other kids without wanting to.

Was this it? Was this what he had to look forward to for the rest of his life?

The nightmare returned, as he knew it would. And *knowing* it was a nightmare didn't make it any better. This time, it was even worse, because there was more to it. It was as if the original nightmare had been an edited version, and he was now seeing a little more.

*   *   *

He is playing in the yard with Ralph. Now he remembers Ralph, as if a locked door in his mind has been shattered by a strong blow and Ralph has escaped.

Ralph is a dog—a huge, playful German shepherd with brown and black fur and a big, happy grin. Ralph loves to roughhouse—growling, nipping, but never hurting. Then, when the game is over, his big, slobbery tongue licks Matt all over his face, arms, and toes. It tickles Matt like crazy when that big pink tongue rasps over the bottom of his feet and in and out of his toes.

Ralph loves him, and he loves Ralph. They are inseparable.

In his dream, Matt again sees the ball roll through the basement door and hears it bounce downstairs. He has to follow it into the dark basement, and this time he knows why—Ralph is down there, and he needs help.

Matt screws up his courage and begins to walk slowly downstairs. Dad has been planning to install several lights in the basement because he is expanding the house down here, but he hasn't gotten around to it yet. A single bulb now hangs from the ceiling. The basement was unfinished when Dad and Mom bought the house. There was just a furnace and water heater, a small laundry room, and some old furniture. The rest was concrete and rough walls. Dad decided that with two kids and a big, playful dog, he needed to build a playroom.

All his tools are down here, and lots of wood and supplies. Dad has been finishing the basement on the weekends. Sometimes he lets Matt help him, but it is usually Penny who gets to do the fun stuff. Matt is kind of clumsy because he is so young. And Ralph is not allowed downstairs. He chewed up some wood once and made Dad mad.

But Ralph is down here now. That is why Matt is going down. Ralph has been downstairs a long time, and Matt doesn't like that.

It is so dark. The single bulb only lights a small area. The rest of the basement is full of shadows. As Matt gets to the bottom of the stairs, he hears Ralph whimpering. Maybe he has hurt himself?

Then the darkness closes around him. He can see the one pool of light in the middle of the floor. In the light is something big and hairy.

There are snarls and growls, and something hits him. Matt screams in his nightmare as he is showered with red, warm, sticky stuff. Then he is hiding,

hiding in the darkness. There is someone here, in the basement. Someone . . .

Someone who has killed Ralph. Who has taken one of the tools from the workbench and murdered poor Ralph. Someone who is angry, and horrible. Someone whose face won't quite come to mind.

And then Penny is on the floor with that awful knife sticking out of her. She is dead and there is blood all over the place, and Uncle Joey's face is full of rage. . . .

*   *   *

Matt suddenly awoke, with that final image of Uncle Joey's angry face burned into his brain. His head felt as if it were going to burst, and there was a scream in his throat fighting to get out. He forced it down with effort. He lay there in his bed, trembling from the horror of the new memories.

He knew who Ralph was now. He had been their dog. Matt had loved Ralph, and Ralph had been utterly devoted to him. There was some fuzziness to his final memories, though. He knew Ralph had been murdered, right before Penny. That's why there was so much blood in the other nightmares! There had been

two killings, not one. But nobody really counted Ralph. He was just a dog. It was always the death of Penny that everyone remembered. Even Matt had forgotten Ralph.

Until tonight.

He fought the pain and fears of his memories, trying to drag out from his terrified mind what had happened that day in the basement. Ralph had gone downstairs. Matt had followed. There was someone there, but he didn't know who. Matt now remembered seeing Ralph jump up at someone, his teeth bared, and murder in his eyes. That had really scared him, because Ralph was the sweetest dog on earth. But the memory of the attack was very real.

Ralph was usually so friendly. Why had he attacked that person? Matt could remember some blows, as if he'd been struck by something. His hands were over his head. That was it.

Then Ralph was dead on the floor, and Matt was hiding. The rest was a blank. What had happened? His conscious mind would not release the full memories of that day. Until this latest nightmare, he'd not even remembered Ralph.

But Uncle Joey did. He must have known that Ralph was Matt's dog. He may even have been trying to scare Matt by mentioning Ralph's name.

But how would he know Matt had been in the basement with Ralph, unless he also had been in the basement with them! Uncle Joey *must* be the murderer!

But his certainty soon collapsed. Uncle Joey had lived next door then. Of course he knew Matt had a dog. He would also have known that both Penny and Ralph had died on the same day in the same way. It really didn't prove anything at all.

There seemed to be nothing but questions in his life right now. That note, for example. How could it have been written in handwriting that was identical to Penny's? Was it possible to make a forgery that good? But who would do such a thing, and why?

He needed to find out more. Much more. He steeled his nerves. The only way he'd get more information was by asking his mother or father. That meant Mom. The murder was a forbidden topic as far as his father was concerned. Both his parents had never gotten over their grief, but his mother was always willing to talk about Penny. Dad, on the other hand, could hardly say her name.

The playroom in the basement was exactly the way it had been on the day of the murder. Dad had lost all interest in finishing it. No one even went down there now.

So it would have to be Mom. She'd cry, but she could at least talk to him about Penny. He'd have to sit through the tears, but he was sure to learn something.

But would it help him—or make the nightmares worse?

4

A Surprise Visitor

He'd brought the subject up after helping his mother clean out a large upstairs closet. She was surprised that he'd offered to help, because he usually avoided work whenever he could. Matt had planned on getting his mother in a good mood, and helping her certainly did that.

The mood changed when he asked about Penny's death. He carefully avoided the word *murder*. Mrs. Howard sighed and put her hand to her head. "Well," she said, finally, "I suppose it was bound to happen. I knew something was bothering you. I don't suppose seeing Uncle Joey again helped much."

Matt thought, *That's an understatement!* His mother led him into the den. She pulled a large scrapbook from the bookshelf there and handed it to him. He had never wanted to look in this book. Something always held him back. Now he opened it up on the table as she stood silently watching him.

It was filled with newspaper clippings about Penny's murder.

It had been quite sensational, clearly. Several front-page stories, and a few longer articles. Then it had faded away, replaced by new tragedies.

There were many pictures of the scene of the crime, and plenty of comments by the neighbors. "What a nice girl she was. It's such a tragedy," one person had said. Another one had commented on the Howards being "such a quiet family. What a shame." They looked like the kinds of comments everyone made when horror-struck.

He wasn't able to find any references to Uncle Joey, even under the name Joe Ciprelli.

Matt already knew most of what he was reading. The only new information came in a story about the investigation. A police spokesman said they had only one suspect. But it wasn't Uncle Joey.

It was his father.

Matt sat back from the book in disbelief. The police had thought his father had killed Penny! It was unthinkable, completely unthinkable. Dad *loved* Penny, and he'd never been the same since her death. Why would anyone think he'd have been capable of killing her? It was impossible.

Except . . .

He heard that little voice in the back of his mind that whispered to him from time to time. It was having a field day now. "How do you *know* Dad didn't kill her?" it asked. "After all, it *would* explain some things. Wouldn't it? Like the fact that he never seems to have any friends come over to visit. Maybe everyone distrusts him."

That wasn't possible! It was just that Dad didn't seem to enjoy anything since Penny died. It was as if he'd lost his own reason for going on with life. And he missed her so much!

"Maybe it's just guilt?" the voice whispered. "If he *did* kill her, then all these years he's been suffering from guilt and fear that he'd be found out."

Matt refused to believe it. His father *hadn't* been the killer! He couldn't have been.

But . . .

"Maybe *that's* why you don't remember what happened," the voice slyly suggested. "If you had seen your own father kill your sister, you might have buried the memory so deeply that it's taken years for it to crawl out again."

No! He wouldn't accept that! He *couldn't*!

Burning with anger and shame at his own doubts, Matt continued to read the report in the newspaper clippings. It turned out that the only reason the police thought Dad might have done it was because it had happened in their basement with his tools. Some sort of wood-working knife had been used to kill both Ralph and Penny. The only prints on it were Penny's, Matt's, and Dad's. No stranger's. And they had all handled the knife when they were doing the work on the basement. Matt was certain he'd never been allowed to use the knife, but he must have at least picked it up at some point.

But there were no signs of any intruder, or anyone else having touched the knife. That *might* rule out Uncle Joey—except he could have gotten into the house without breaking in. Maybe he'd worn gloves, and that was why his fingerprints weren't on the knife. Or would that have smudged the other prints? Matt really didn't know. But he was certain that Uncle Joey was far more likely to have killed Penny than Dad was.

The police had never arrested his dad, which proved—what? "Only that they couldn't make the case stick," the suspicious voice told him. "And what did that prove? Not that Dad was innocent, just that they couldn't prove he was guilty. He was never cleared of the murder— just never accused in court."

Matt was confused and uncertain. The more he learned, the less it seemed he knew.

He stared at his mother. Tears were trickling down her cheeks. "It's not true, is it?" he whispered. "About Dad . . ."

"No!" she said, fiercely. "The police just

said that because they had no suspects. They were afraid of looking stupid if they didn't suspect *someone*. So they picked on your father. It still hurts him, after all these years, Matt. It was a horrible thing to be accused of. You can't imagine."

Matt nodded. "Who . . . who do *you* think did it?" he asked her.

She shrugged. "Some stranger. Someone trying to rob the house while your father and I were out. That's all. But the police never found any clues."

Nervously, he said: "You don't think . . ." He swallowed, and went on: "You don't think Uncle Joey could have done it?"

"Him?" His mother gave a brittle laugh. "No, Matt. He *adored* your sister. He always told us he wished he'd gotten married when he'd had the chance and had a daughter like her. They were always together. When Penny . . . died, he broke down completely. Started talking nonsense, claiming he'd seen things. Then they locked him away."

"Things?" echoed Matt. "What sort of things?"

"Oh, nothing important," his mother replied, just a little too quickly to be believable. Then she closed the book and replaced it on the shelf. "That's enough." She wiped her eyes with a tissue.

Matt left the house on his bike. Mom was lying to him; that much was clear. Whatever Uncle Joey had seen was important enough to make him go crazy, at least for a while. Why had she lied about it, then? Why wouldn't she tell him the whole story?

Without thinking about it consciously, he found himself going back to the cemetery. It was as if something were drawing him to the place.

He hesitated at the gates. He very rarely came here. And he didn't know why he was here now. But in his heart there seemed to be something tugging at him, dragging him into the cemetery. He didn't really want to go in, but he couldn't bring himself to head home. In the end he chained his bike to a post and set off through the silent gravestones.

A feeling of calm settled over Matt as he walked. The cemetery was so quiet and peaceful today. It *was* a fine and private place indeed, and it seemed to speak to him and soothe his soul. Somehow the worries about the nightmare and Uncle Joey drifted away here.

He walked over to Penny's grave. He didn't have anything in mind except to visit it again. There could hardly be any change since he had been here last.

He could not have been more wrong.

As soon as he saw the grave, he stopped and stared at it in shock.

The flowers he'd brought two days ago were scattered across the grass, ripped into pieces. One of the grounds keepers was gathering them up, tossing them into a plastic bag. As Matt hurried over, the man looked at him, annoyed because he had extra work to do.

"Do you know who did this?" the grounds keeper asked suspiciously.

"No!" Matt said, shaking his head. "That's my sister's grave. I brought the flowers a couple of days ago. What happened?"

"Vandals, I guess," the man muttered. "Look at what they've done." He gave Matt a dark stare. "There are some funny types in here, if you know what I mean." He tapped the side of his head. "Real crazies, you know? Think it's funny to destroy things."

A horrible suspicion was forming in Matt's mind. "Have you seen an old man here?" he asked. "Sort of half-shaved—walks stooped over?"

"Plenty of them," the man answered.

So Uncle Joey *might* have been here. . . . Matt didn't know whether it helped to have this information. Would he have destroyed the flowers like this? Matt had no doubt that the old man was capable of it, but why would he do such a thing?

The grounds keeper paused as he worked. "Your sister's grave, you say?" he asked, giving Matt another suspicious look.

"Yes." Matt glared at him, angry that the guy didn't believe him.

"Well," the man told him, "there's more been done to it."

A chill went up and down Matt's spine. "More?" he echoed. "What more?"

The man pointed to the grass. "Look there."

Matt stared at the grass. It had been disturbed, he now saw. There were rips in the turf, and some of the bare earth underneath was exposed. He bent down for a better look.

The way it was, it looked as if the ground had been disturbed by something *underneath*. As though something—or someone—had pushed up from under the ground.

"You look as if you've seen a ghost, son," the grounds keeper remarked. He didn't seem quite so angry now. "Maybe you'd better sit down before you fall down." He nodded to one of the benches nearby. "Go on."

In a daze, Matt did as he was told. His head was spinning. He felt slightly ill. All these things, one after another, were more than he could handle. He had to have time to sort out his thoughts.

The grave looked exactly as if Penny had pushed up out of it and torn the flowers to shreds herself. Of course, that was impossible. Wasn't it? Things like that didn't happen.

When you were dead, you were dead. That was it.

Corpses only got up and walked the night in horror films. Not in real life.

Penny was dead and ten years buried.

Then he saw the shadow. It fell across the

path in front of him, and he jumped. He thought it was the grounds keeper, coming to see how he was.

He glanced up. He could feel the blood drain from his face.

It was Penny.

Wait a minute. It wasn't *really* Penny. It was that girl again, the one he'd seen a couple of days ago here at the cemetery and then again at school. The one that looked so much like his sister. It wasn't Penny. There was no way it could be.

But she looked as though she was about ten or eleven years old, the age Penny had been when she died. And she had Penny's straight blond hair, and the same intense blue eyes. And she looked so neat and precise, just as Penny always had.

"Who . . . ?" he began. His voice came out as an embarrassing squeak. He swallowed, but his throat was so dry that he almost gagged. "Who *are* you?" he finally managed to ask.

"I'm Penny." She stared coldly at him. "And I've come to talk to you."

5

Revenge

"No!" Matt stared at her, refusing to accept what she said. But on another, deeper level, he was convinced that she was telling the truth. She *couldn't* be Penny! But . . .

Penny, back from the dead, to haunt him!

"You can't be a ghost!" he told her. Maybe if he *tried* to believe that, she'd vanish.

She laughed, scornfully. "I'm not a ghost," she replied. She took a step forward, then reached down and pinched his bare arm. It hurt, and he pulled back. "And you're not dreaming, either," she added. "So, now that we've eliminated all the usual silly conversation, can we get on to the really important stuff?"

Matt felt as if he were being sucked into a whirlpool of madness. This was getting too crazy! How could this girl say she was Penny, but not be a ghost? "What do you want?" he asked. Then, he challenged her forcefully: "Who are you, *really*?"

The girl sighed. "This is going to be every bit as difficult as I expected." She shook her head. "You're just as stupid as you were when I died. Move over."

Matt moved quickly to one side on the seat. Penny—the girl, or whatever she was—sat beside him, her hands folded demurely in her lap. He thought it seemed just the way his sister would've sat.

"You've heard of reincarnation, haven't you?" she asked him suddenly.

He nodded. "Yeah. That's like when after you die, you come back in another body and start life over. . . ." His voice trailed off as he stared at her. "You mean . . . ?"

Penny rolled her eyes. "Yes, I'm your sister, Penny, reincarnated in this body."

"But that's *crazy!*" Matt cried.

"*You're* the one that's crazy," she snapped back. "Reincarnation has been around forever. Millions of people believe in it. Why is it so hard for you to accept?"

Matt shook his head, trying to fight the idea. But it seemed strangely believable. "It's one of those dumb things they discuss on talk shows," he said. "It's never been proven."

"*I'm* proving it—right now," the girl said. "I can tell you anything you like about you and your house and your parents—up to the time I was murdered, of course. Ask me anything you like. I remember it all."

Matt could see that she was serious. He still didn't want to believe it, though. It was just too hard to accept that this could be his dead sister, alive and in a new body that was almost a duplicate of her old one. "I can't ask much," he said, glumly. "I was only four when you died. I can't remember anything myself, re-ally."

"You're making this very difficult," she complained. "You really must believe that I'm

Penny, back from the dead. It's very important."

He frowned at her. "But if—and I mean *if*—you're reincarnated, then how come you actually remember your past life as my sister? I mean, if we *do* get reincarnated, doesn't that mean that I was once somebody else? How come I can't remember that, and yet you can remember being Penny?"

"You'd forget your own name if it wasn't sewn into your gym shorts," the girl sneered. "But, if you must know, I only remembered being Penny a little over a year ago." She pushed back the hair on the side of her head. There was a slight scar on her temple. It was white, even against her pale skin. "I fell down and hit my head hard on a post. When I woke up in the hospital, I remembered all about my past life—and death."

Matt was chilled again. "Penny had a scar right there," he whispered. "And she got it—"

"—from falling down the basement stairs," the girl finished. "Yes, I remembered that part, too."

She knew about *that*. . . . Matt was losing his battle against believing her. "You left the

newspaper article and poem on your grave,"
he said. "And wrote me that note."

"Of course I did."

In Penny's handwriting . . . "I don't know,"
he said miserably. "It's just too wacko to believe. But . . ."

"But there isn't any other explanation. Is
there?" She glanced down at her watch.
"Look, I can't hang around here all day talking
to you. I'll give you a day or so to think about
things. I have something special I want you to
do for me. But you must believe that I'm your
sister. Can you meet me here on Friday, say
around ten in the morning?" She stood up to
leave.

"But—*why*?" he demanded, jumping to his
feet. "Why are you here? Why are you doing
this to me?"

"Because the person who killed me was
never caught and punished," the girl told him.
"Because I was murdered and I want revenge." She looked deeply into his eyes. Matt
trembled in the face of her stare. "But you
don't remember, do you?" She shook her head
in answer to her own question. "You've buried

the memories of my murder. Well, I can't do anything without your help. You *must* remember what you saw that day! It's vital!''

Matt stared at her helplessly. "So I really did see you get killed," he said slowly. He didn't just find Penny's body, as his parents had said. His nightmares were what really had happened!

"Oh, yes," she told him. "You saw everything. But you've forgotten it." She grabbed his arm. Her fingers were like steel rods, pressing into his skin. "You *must* remember!" Then she let him go, leaving white marks where her fingers had clutched him.

"Can't you just tell me?" he asked her.

"No," she replied. "It has to come from within you. It's the only way. Try to remember. I'll see you again on Friday." She turned around and walked quickly away, never looking back.

Matt stood speechless, watching her leave. Was it possible that she was telling the truth? Could it really be that she was Penny, reincarnated? Did she really need his help in catching her own killer?

He was no longer sure of anything. He'd always believed that life ended here, in the graveyard. Once you were dead, that was it. Ashes to ashes, dust to dust . . . He'd never been able to believe in any kind of God or afterlife. But if this girl was telling the truth, the graveyard was simply a recycling center— the bodies returned to the ground, the souls moved on, turned into new human beings somewhere else.

He needed to know more about this strange girl. She might claim to be his sister, but she had another life now. He had to follow her, find out where she lived, who she really was. The idea of *doing* something gave him fresh confidence. He sprinted down the path she'd taken—not the one he'd come by, but one leading to a side entrance. He caught sight of her again ahead of him. She didn't look back, but he didn't want to take any chances. He was certain that she wouldn't be pleased if she saw him, so he kept to the side of the path. If she happened to look back, he could quickly duck out of sight. But she kept on walking in a straight line, obviously with a firm purpose in mind. His parents often spoke of how determined Penny had always been. Once she made up her mind to do something, there was no changing it or stopping her.

Matt was bombarded by so many emotions and questions that he hardly knew what to focus on. If this *was* his sister, shouldn't he be happy that she wasn't *really* dead? Then why was it so hard to believe? And why didn't he want to believe her story? Maybe he should tell his parents that this girl was their beloved Penny. But would it help them, or would it turn them against him? Would they think he was making a joke out of Penny's death?

Matt wondered why Penny couldn't just *tell* him who had killed her. No, he realized, trailing through the streets behind her. That wouldn't work. If she wanted to put her killer in jail, she'd have to have proof that would stand up in court. Matt was certain that no jury would ever believe that this girl was the victim reincarnated. If *he* was doubting, they'd certainly never believe. So . . . if he *had* seen her killed, as she said, he'd be able to identify the killer.

If he could remember who the killer was.

The girl finally turned onto Thorne Road. He knew the area vaguely. He'd once had a friend a couple of blocks from here, but they'd had a big fight. The girl headed for a small house on the corner. It was a nice split-level, and there were windows showing that it had a basement. There was a chain-link fence that ran all around the yard. The mailbox out front had a number and name on it, but he was too far away to read them. When the girl went through the front door, he hurried along faster. He would just casually walk by the mailbox. At least then he could find out what the girl's name was.

The number on the mailbox was 67. Under it, in smaller letters, was the name: GILLIS. Matt stopped, staring at the word.

In a whirlwind of motion, something slammed into the fence, barking furiously. Matt jumped back, shocked. It was a large German shepherd, and it looked a lot like the dog in the nightmare.

"Ralph . . ." he whispered.

The dog *did* look uncannily like Ralph, though this one was snarling and growling and looked as if it wanted to attack. Knowing it could be dangerous, he reached his hand over the fence. Many dogs would bite a stranger who did that, and this one looked like a tough guard dog.

The big dog jumped up, but instead of biting Matt, it licked his hand. Matt could remember Ralph licking him that way. He glanced at the house. Out of the corner of his eye he saw the curtain move slightly in the window by the door. He looked up and saw the girl staring back at him. The dog licked him again. Matt decided it was time to go. What would he say if she came outside?

On the next block, an elderly lady was watching him from her own yard. Matt's heart started to beat faster, as if he had done something wrong. Did she think he was a trouble-maker? As he walked by the house, though, she smiled at him. Relieved, he grinned back.

"I've never seen old Pueblo so worked up," the woman said to him. "He's generally a nasty critter." She stood up from the pad she'd been kneeling on to plant geraniums. Dusting off her knees, she gave him another smile. "Still, he's probably just taken a shine to you."

"I suppose," Matt agreed. "I had a dog like him once myself."

The old woman looked at him thoughtfully. "I know why you look so jumpy," she said. "It's the old teenage problem." She gave him a wink. "Got a crush on young Penny Gillis, have you?"

Her name really was Penny! He was even more confused now. Was this just another co-incidence, or did it mean something? Matt stood there speechless. The old lady smiled at him.

"Nothing to be ashamed of," she told him. "As long as you always bear in mind that you have to respect the girls, young man." Then she smiled again, taking the sting from her words. "And, confidentially, we ladies *always* appreciate attention."

"She's kinda young," Matt finally managed to say. "And I'm not really—"

"Pretty, though." It was clear the old woman had her own ideas and wasn't about to let go of them easily. "She'll be a beauty when she grows up. You just wait and see."

Matt excused himself and ran off. That was all he needed! He'd been honest with the old

woman—his interest in Penny wasn't because
he liked her! For one thing, he wasn't inter-
ested in *anyone*, at least not that way. For another, even if he were, he'd pick an older girl,
someone nearer his own age. And he'd pick
someone who hadn't been his sister in her past
life!

With a start, Matt realized that he had ac-
cepted Penny Gillis's story. Wild as it was,
there didn't seem to be any other answer: this
was his sister, Penny, back again in a new
life. And with a notion to get revenge for her
murder.

And, buried somewhere in the depths of his
own mind, he must know. But would he ever
remember it all?

Matt walked back to the cemetery to get his
bike and head home.

As he got on the bike, he saw a flash of
movement out of the corner of his eye. He
waited for a few minutes, but whatever was
there didn't reappear.

Matt couldn't be absolutely certain, but he

thought he'd seen a man, a man who looked a lot like Uncle Joey. Was the old man following him? Matt had *thought* several times this week that someone had been watching him when he was out, though he'd never actually seen anyone. He had tried to tell himself that he was making it all up, that he was just spooked by this Penny business.

But maybe he was right. Maybe Uncle Joey really *was* following him.

Matt shivered as he pedaled faster on his bike. He remembered Uncle Joey's angry face from his dream the night before. Matt was almost positive that Uncle Joey had been in the basement the day that Penny was killed. That didn't make the old man a murderer, but he sure *seemed* guilty.

As Matt turned into his driveway, he got a queasy feeling in the pit of his stomach. If Uncle Joey murdered his sister, he must have known that Matt was also in the basement and could have seen the whole thing. Maybe Uncle Joey was just trying to keep tabs on Matt by watching him at home and following him around town to see if he would go to the police. Or maybe Uncle Joey had a more drastic—and permanent—solution in mind.

He looked over at the old man's house. The rocking chair on Uncle Joey's front porch was empty, and for the first time in days Matt couldn't see him at any of the windows.

Maybe I'm next, Matt thought.

Matt dreaded going to bed now. As a kid, bed had always been a warm and cozy place to be. It had been fun to snuggle under the covers and go to sleep. But since the nightmares had started, it was now a place of horror for Matt. He knew that as soon as he fell asleep, he'd begin to dream. But he couldn't stay awake forever. And, as much as he wanted answers to all the questions about Penny's murder, he wasn't sure he could face up to them in his nightmares.

He lay on his back in the dark, trying to keep his tired eyelids open. It was no use. Though he fought against it, sleep was coming, and along with it came—

—the darkness.

*   *   *

Matt is small again, a four-year-old at the top of the basement stairs. Dad always said that he should never go down alone. But he isn't alone. Ralph ran downstairs moments ago, following the ball they had been playing with.

"Ralph!" calls Matt. "Come here, doggie!" But there is no reply. Maybe Ralph is sick?

Slowly, carefully, Matt grabs hold of the stair railing and starts to climb down into the basement. It takes him awhile, because his legs are so small. Below he can see a small circle of light in the middle of the floor.

There is a noise, a kind of slamming sound, and then Ralph barks sharply in pain.

"Ralph!" cries Matt, scared for his very best friend. "Come here, Ralph!"

The next part is still fuzzy. There is a movement in the shadows, a shape he can't quite make out. Then suddenly he is slammed against the wall. He hurts all over, but something even worse is happening.

Matt yells in terror. Ralph leaps at a strange, shadowy form, and then Matt sees a huge knife raised high above the dog. The blade bites deeply into Ralph's side, and blood splatters all over. Some of it splashes on him, and he screams.

Then he runs to hide in the darkness, where the knife can't find him.

His heart is pounding in terror as he hides. The next thing he knows, Penny is on the floor with the knife sticking straight out of her. Her blood runs down her white clothing, pooling on the floor with Ralph's. There is some of it on Matt, too, and he screams and screams.

His hand is on the knife.

There is a noise at one of the basement windows, and he looks up.

There, framed in the window, is the shocked face of Uncle Joey.

He is outside, not in the basement.

*   *   *

Matt jerked upright in bed, shivering despite the damp heat of the night. He was breathing in gasps, and his heart was hammering away. Gradually, he calmed down. A little light crept in through the curtains. He looked down at his hands, as if he expected to see blood on them. They were gray in the dim morning light, but clean. He didn't have Penny's blood on them.

Penny's blood . . .

He lay back down, trying to force the images out of his mind, but they refused to go. He could see his hands on the knife that killed Penny. Had *he* done it? Was *he* the killer? Had Uncle Joey seen him by her body, kneeling in her blood?

Matt had begun to believe that Uncle Joey was the killer. It was one of the few theories that made sense. Now he knew he'd been wrong. Uncle Joey had been outside looking through the basement window when Penny was killed.

He couldn't remember anyone else in the dream. Just him, Penny, Ralph and Uncle Joey. And Ralph was dead; Penny was dead; and Uncle Joey was on the outside, looking in.

That left only one possible murderer.

6

Dead Dog

"Was it really me?" Matt whispered. He was all mixed up now. To try to relax a little, he'd gone out into the yard after breakfast. Normally he would sit under a tree and watch the sunlight filter through the leaves. It was a soothing place to be, but not today. Nothing could calm his nerves.

Had he killed Penny?

It all seemed so simple just a day or so ago. Some maniac—or maybe even Uncle Joey—

had broken into the house and killed his sister. He had hidden, and when the killer was gone he was the first one to find the body.

Now that didn't seem possible. There *was* no maniac. And he might have been the first to find Penny's body because he'd killed her himself.

And Uncle Joey had seen him do it.

Matt realized now what was haunting the old man next door. He hadn't been trying to keep tabs on Matt—or kill him—to cover up his own guilt. He'd been watching and waiting for Matt to make a slip, so that he could prove Matt was a killer. . . . And that had to have been the "impossible" thing he claimed to have seen. That was what his mother and the police refused to believe. And what had finally gotten Uncle Joey locked up as a mental case.

But he still couldn't remember doing it. The dreams had revealed much of what happened that day, but there was still much he didn't know. The murder was like a jigsaw puzzle, and he'd put together enough pieces to get some idea of the final picture. But he knew, instinctively, that it wasn't at all finished.

There was a big area still blank, and he had no idea what might be lurking there.

Now he could remember touching the knife after Penny was dead. But he'd been a child. Maybe he hadn't stabbed her but just tried to take it out, as if it would make her well again. Kids did try to do silly things like that. Or was he just trying to convince himself that he couldn't have murdered Penny? He didn't *feel* like a killer.

But what did a killer feel like?

Desperately, he tried to get all the facts together. Okay, he *had* been there during the murder. And it *did* look pretty bad for him, even if only he and Uncle Joey saw what happened. After all, nobody seemed to have suspected him of the killing.

Or did they?

It was clear to Matt now that Uncle Joey was convinced that he had killed Penny. The old man *must* have said so at the time of the murder. But Matt guessed that no one had actually believed him, because nothing had come of the accusation. But maybe, just *maybe*, Mom and Dad believed that Matt had killed his sister, too. It would explain why they were so cold toward him—why things had turned out so badly after the murder. Even if they didn't consciously blame him, there had to be that nagging doubt in their minds.

Maybe that was why they had never gotten over Penny's death. And why they constantly praised her and put Matt down. Maybe they were striking back at him for killing her, even though they had no proof and weren't certain he'd really done it. The suspicion would have been enough to turn them against him.

He felt terrible. Even if he were innocent, things couldn't get better. Unless he could discover who had *really* killed Penny. What if he hadn't done it? There were only two people who could help him find out if he was the killer.

Penny herself. And Uncle Joey.

Matt glanced across at his neighbor's house. The curtain was swaying slightly in the window. The old man must have been watching him again.

Did he have the courage to go over and talk to Uncle Joey? He'd been avoiding the old man

ever since he'd arrived. He still didn't trust
Uncle Joey, but did that even matter now?

What was best—to avoid the truth or to
know it? Matt wished he could decide. If the
truth was that he'd killed Penny, did he really
want to know it? Would he be able to live with
himself if he discovered that he'd killed his
own sister?

But most confusing was *why* he would do
such a thing. Did he have a reason for killing
her? Didn't he love her?

He actually wasn't certain. He knew broth-
ers were supposed to love their sisters. And
he did feel an ache inside of him when he
thought about her being dead. But his feelings
were mixed sometimes. Maybe it was just because he'd been so young and didn't really
understand what it meant to love someone.

Or maybe he had never *wanted* to love her.
Face facts, he told himself, ashamed. *You pick
fights with almost all of your friends.* That was the
truth. He did seem to have ended many of his
friendships. Maybe there was just something
inside of him that made him grow to hate other
people. And it came out sometimes, like when

he was so angry he'd beaten up Laney Mills. He didn't even know why he'd done it. It had gotten him into serious trouble at the time, mostly because he'd punched a girl.

Had he done that to his sister? Had he flown into some mad rage and killed her? Then, to cover up his own guilt, had he locked the memory of the event away so deeply in his mind it was only now breaking free?

He stared at Uncle Joey's house again. No, he couldn't face the old man. How could he? It was obvious what *he* believed—that Matt was a killer who'd never been punished.

Matt wondered what he should do. Suppose—just suppose—he did eventually remember killing Penny. Would he give himself up to the police and confess? Or would he try to bury it again and live as if nothing had ever happened? Even if he had killed Penny, it was ten years ago, and he'd been a kid. He would never do something like that again. Not now. He wasn't the murdering type.

The picture of Laney Mills flashed into his mind again. He'd given her a bloody nose and could remember standing in front of her with blood on his knuckles. And he couldn't even remember why he'd done it.

He didn't like the gaps in his memory. It was almost as if something were lurking inside him, carefully removing the parts he wouldn't want to remember.

But he *had* to know the truth. He wasn't sure what he would do once he knew it. He wasn't sure if he'd like himself at all when he was done. But it was the torture of not being certain that tore him apart. At whatever cost to himself, he *must* know what happened that day in the basement.

So he had to go see Penny again.

She'd promised to meet him at the cemetery on Friday, but this was Thursday. He'd have to try to find her at her home. She could answer his questions.

And if she wouldn't? What would he do then? Force her to talk?

Hit her? *Make* her tell?

Relive the murder all over again?

No! He couldn't do that. He'd just have to beg her to tell him. Nothing more than that. He promised himself. If she wouldn't tell him, then he'd have to live with it somehow. He wouldn't get violent.

He *wouldn't*.

His courage began crumbling once he reached Thorne Road. Was this *really* a smart move?

Did he have any other choice but to try?

A block before the Gillis house, he got off his bike and pushed it slowly beside him as he walked the rest of the way. He knew he was only trying to delay things. He couldn't help it. His insides were twisted up by nerves and a fear of what he might discover.

Then Matt stopped dead in his tracks.

There was a police car parked beside the house. Its lights were flashing but the siren was silent.

For a second, panic filled him and he wanted to run. Then his mind took over and fought down the fear. Whatever the police car was doing here, it couldn't have anything to do with him. He didn't have to run or hide.

What was he so scared of? He hadn't done anything!

Except maybe murder his only sister.

What if Penny had called the police and told them he'd killed her? They might be after him now!

No, that was crazy. He was just getting weirded out, suspicious of everyone and everything. Penny couldn't have done that. She had no proof that she was Penny Howard reincarnated. The police would just laugh at her if she told them that. They'd never believe he was a killer.

Anyway, he *wasn't* a killer.

The policeman was in the car, writing something on a pad. Matt stood there, wondering whether or not to ask what had happened. Could he look at the guy without having it seem that he was involved in any way?

The decision was taken out of his hands. With a roar, the police car pulled away and drove off. The flashing lights on top of the car went dead. The policeman's business at the Gillis house was done for now.

Matt felt a sense of relief. At least he didn't

have that to face at the moment. No police. No trial, or jail. But maybe no answers, either.

He stopped at the gate. What was he going to do? Stand here all day, building up enough courage to go in? Or would he just run away, forgetting his need for answers in case they were ones he didn't like?

For the second time, the decision was made for him. The door to the Gillis house flew open, and a woman stepped outside. Matt jumped, as if he were doing something wrong by standing there.

"Who are you?" the woman snapped. "Why have you been lurking around our house?"

Matt swallowed and stared at her. This had to be Penny's mom—her new mom, that was. She did look kind of like Penny, with fair hair and the same sort of features. It was obvious that Penny would soon have a brother or sister. One of Mrs. Gillis's hands rested on her very pregnant stomach. The other gripped the doorjamb.

"Uh . . ." he began, his voice faint. "Uh, I came to talk to Penny, please."

Mrs. Gillis's eyes narrowed, and she looked at him suspiciously. "Who are you?" she repeated. "You're not from around here, are you?"

"My name's Terry Wayne," Matt lied, feebly. "Penny knows me." He hated standing at the gate like this. He wondered if Penny's dog was outside somewhere, as it had been yesterday. But he didn't dare take his eyes off the woman to look for it. She might be even more hostile if she thought he was acting shifty. And he didn't know why he'd given her the name of one of the other boys in his class. Was he covering his tracks, just in case? In case of what?

Mrs. Gillis seemed to soften slightly. He could tell she wasn't usually a grumpy person. But the police had been here, and it looked as though something were wrong. "I don't think this is a good time to talk to her," she said.

"Oh." Matt couldn't think of anything else to say. "Uh—why not?"

"If you must know," Mrs. Gillis said, "we found Pueblo dead this morning."

The dog? Wasn't that the dog's name? Matt swallowed hard. He felt his fingers tighten on the fence. Mrs. Gillis glared at him suspiciously again.

"You wouldn't happen to know anything about it, would you?" she asked.

"No!" he blurted out. "I'd never kill a dog."

That did it.

"How did you know he was killed?" Mrs. Gillis asked sharply. She stared at him with open hostility now. "Are you sure you don't know anything about it? What did you say your name was again? Terry Something?"

Why *had* he said that? Surely it was just because he was thinking about Ralph. Wasn't it? Ralph had been killed; that was all. He didn't know *anything* about Pueblo's death. But he had seen the police car. It was just a guess that had happened to have been right.

But he couldn't say any of this to Mrs. Gillis. Instead, he jumped on his bike and pedaled madly away until he was a few blocks from the house. When he calmed down and started thinking instead of panicking, he realized that he was in front of the cemetery again.

It was odd how lately he always seemed to end up here. He locked his bike outside and then walked quickly toward Penny's grave.

He forced himself to slow down and walk at a normal pace. If he looked as panicked as he felt, he could attract attention. He had to get a grip on himself. He'd done enough stupid things for one day. Running away from Mrs. Gillis like that! How could he have been so *dumb*? She must be certain now that he was involved in killing their dog.

What if she called the police and reported him? He'd given her a fake name! But the police would track him down somehow—all they had to do was have Mrs. Gillis look over the kids in his class. He hadn't killed the dog, but he was sure it would be hard to prove it. And he couldn't even explain to himself why he'd given a false name. That would make him look even more guilty! What sort of things did they do with kids who killed dogs, anyway? Would he just get a warning? Or would he be sent to some kind of reform school? Would he be taken away from Mom and Dad?

Slow down! he said to himself. This is ridiculous! He was acting as if he were guilty. And he wasn't.

He'd just panicked when Mrs. Gillis questioned him. He hadn't done anything wrong. The police would believe him.

"Right," a voice inside him said. "And what will you say when they ask you to tell them *why* you were at the house just now? *I wanted to ask their daughter if I really killed my sister?* Now that's sure to get their sympathy! And when they ask why you lied about your name—then what?"

He tried not to listen to this, but it was impossible to shut it out. It didn't make any difference, really, whether he'd done anything wrong or not. It certainly looked pretty bad for him.

"Don't be so scared," the voice whispered. "You didn't even tell her your real name. She can't turn you in to the cops."

Right! "Terry Something," she'd called him. He was okay. There had to be a dozen Terrys in town. They'd never think he did it. He was safe. Why was he torturing himself like this? He had nothing to hide. So he had nothing to be scared of.

It was all so terrible, so confusing. He threw himself onto the closest piece of grass and tried to quiet his frantic thoughts. He had to relax. He had to find some peace. Like here among the graves.

But it wasn't as peaceful as he'd once believed. Penny wasn't dead and quiet. She was back again and very much a part of his life. Maybe there was no rest for anyone, not even in the grave. The graveyard was like a landfill, only here the trash wasn't lawn clippings, baby diapers, and rotting food. It was discarded bodies, their souls having moved on to new places. There was no peace, not even in death.

Something moved by the cemetery gate. Matt tensed. For a second, he thought it was the police, after him for killing Pueblo. Then reason returned and he listened carefully. It was simply a hearse driving in. Another day, another funeral.

He shook his head, sadly. Once he had envied the dead their rest and peace. Now he realized how foolish that had been. This wasn't so much a place to sleep in death. It was more like a busy train station, where the souls of the dearly departed moved on to some other life, some other destination.

There were no answers here. Matt wearily got to his feet and slowly walked back to where he'd left his bike. He wondered if he'd find answers anywhere.

7

Catching a Killer

There was a knock at his door. Joey Ciprelli jumped, then remembered who it had to be. He moved slowly to the door. Though it was summer, he felt a chill in his bones. He couldn't move very quickly anymore. He couldn't do a lot of things that he'd once been able to do. Ten years was a long time to be in the hospital. He'd drifted while he was in there. He'd been treated like a crazy man and he'd lost the will to care.

Until recently.

He opened the door, and young Penny Gillis slipped quickly inside. "Nobody saw you. Did they?" he asked urgently.

"No." She flashed him a wonderful, easy smile. Just the way that Penny Howard had always smiled. If he hadn't known better, he could have mistaken the two girls for one; they looked so alike. "Anyway, Matt's too wrapped up in his memories to see anything that's happening now."

"Maybe," Joey agreed. "But we've come so far. I'd hate to have any part of the plan go wrong just when we've almost got him."

"It won't," she promised him. She rested one of her pale hands on his arm. "You've worked it out wonderfully, Uncle Joey. We'll make him pay for what he did."

"You're a good girl, Penny," he told her affectionately. "Just like the first Penny."

"I guess she and I would have had a lot in common," Penny Gillis replied. "That's why it has been so easy to fool Matt."

"Yes." Joey smiled. "I remember the shock I got when I first saw you." He was lost in his memories now. It was hard simply to walk away from ten years in Brookville Hospital. He'd almost been glad when they'd taken him there, away from this house. Nobody had believed him when he told the police he'd seen young Matt Howard kill his older sister. They said that a four-year-old boy couldn't have done such a horrible thing. But he'd known what he'd seen. That boy was a monster, a demon, a real bad seed. There was no way he could just keep quiet about the murder. Finally, the neighbors thought he needed help. That's why he was sent to Brookville.

He'd let those years in the hospital wash away a lot of his strength. He couldn't fight them. He'd done whatever the doctors and psychiatrists had asked. He never forgot the murder, though, or Matt. But he'd just drifted, letting whatever happened slide right over him. Then, a year ago, the doctors suggested he start writing to a pen pal. One of the social studies classes at a local school had started a program for the students to write to the elderly or to people in hospitals. He'd agreed to take part, or rather, he hadn't argued with the doctors when they gave him a letter from a young girl named Penny.

It must have been the name that reminded him of poor Penny Howard, because he took an interest in this girl and decided to write back. They had corresponded even after Penny's class was over. Finally, she'd come to see him on his birthday. She showed up at the hospital with her parents and a cake.

At that moment, he hatched the plot to trap Matt. And he set his mind to getting released from the hospital. With a new reason to live, his spirits picked up. He made every effort to get along with the doctors and nurses, and he worked hard to get certified as sane. He convinced the hospital staff that he was all better, and finally he was a free man. But only Penny knew why he *really* wanted to be out. She had agreed to help him.

Joey was certain that he could convince Matt that Penny Gillis was his sister, Penny, reincarnated. He coached the new Penny in the ways of his old favorite. Every move, every word, every mannerism of Penny's was etched in his mind. He'd had little else to think about for ten years. Penny learned quickly, and she had a remarkable memory for everything he told her about the murdered girl.

Now they were ready for the last step.

"I'm still amazed that Matt believes this garbage about my being Penny Howard reborn," Penny said, sitting down on a shabby couch in Joey's living room. "I mean, it's just so wild. Isn't it?"

"He's got a guilty conscience," Joey replied. "The guilt has been building in his mind since he killed her. Now, I have a way to prove I wasn't crazy ten years ago. And between the two of us, we'll see that he's finally punished for what he did."

He picked up a small tape recorder from the coffee table in front of the couch. "This is how we'll catch him. I want you to slip the tape recorder into your purse before you meet with Matt tomorrow. It will pick up every word of your conversation about the murder. Then we'll have a taped confession."

Penny gave him another dazzling smile. "Okay!" she said excitedly. "Tomorrow, I'll get him talking. Then we can go to the police with the tape."

"You're not afraid, are you?" he asked her. "I mean, he might get violent if he thinks you really *are* his sister. He killed you once—I mean, he killed the other Penny. I can't pretend it might not be dangerous. But I won't be far away, and after about half an hour I'll come over and check up on you. I'm not as strong as I used to be, but I can still help if anything goes wrong."

"I'll be careful," she promised. Penny got up from the couch and grasped Joey's withered old hand tightly. "I'm not afraid. You've gone through so much pain because of him. We *have* to get him. You're sure he's going to break down?"

"Yes." Joey smiled grimly at Penny's earnest face. "I've been watching him. He's ready." He handed her the tape recorder. "And now so are we. When you see him tomorrow, I guarantee we'll get what we're after—and he'll finally get what he deserves."

As if Matt didn't feel awful enough, for some reason his father was grouchy all evening. He arrived home late from work in a bad mood. Dinner didn't suit him, and he snapped at Mom. Then Mom started her

"nobody-around-here-appreciates-me" speech and stormed out of the kitchen. Since Matt was the only one left, his dad yelled at him.

"Your mother's right," he snapped. "You *don't* appreciate what she does for you." Matt almost choked on his dinner—she'd been talking about *Dad*, not him! His father picked up a sweatshirt that Matt had dropped on a chair when he came in. "Look at this—do you think your mother has nothing better to do than clean up after you?" He tossed the shirt to Matt. "Put it in the dirty laundry where it belongs! And while you're at it, pick up the dirty stuff on the floor in your room. Your sister never left her room in a mess. *She* was organized and finished a job once she began it. Why don't you try doing the same?"

Though he was stung by the injustice of the attack, Matt knew better than to argue with his dad when he was in one of his moods. He'd probably had a bad day at work or something and was taking it out on anyone within striking distance. And Matt was a real sitting duck.

He threw the sweatshirt into the bathroom hamper, then slowly started to gather up the rest of the clothes scattered around his room. At least it gave him something to focus on, instead of the Penny business. He wasn't sure that Mom would consider this help, however. He was filling the basket pretty quickly, which meant she'd have to do laundry.

The comparison with his sister hurt Matt. She'd been dead for ten years, and still they kept telling him how wonderful she was. She really was perfect. She even kept her room clean, as if that were the greatest accomplishment in the history of the world. Big deal! Something that Dad had said stuck in Matt's mind, though: that she always finished a job once she started it. Was that what she was doing now? Finishing the job of bringing her killer to justice?

Was it *he* she was after? She had said that she couldn't do anything unless he remembered. He'd thought she meant he had to remember who the killer was. But maybe she meant that he had to remember that *he* had killed her.

He wished he knew what had really happened that day. Why couldn't he remember?

Eventually, the evening ended, and it was

time to go to bed. Matt tried to put it off, but his dad was still in a bad mood. "You need your sleep," he said at eleven. "I certainly need mine. Bed—*now!*"

Left with no choice, Matt crawled under his blanket. He knew that the nightmares would be back and that they would not let him rest. Terrifying thoughts of death, blood, the police, and his sister's face haunted him as he lay in the stillness, waiting to fall asleep.

What had he done? What had he done?

If only he could talk to his parents about his fears. He needed someone to comfort him and tell him everything would be all right. But they'd never understand. They never understood *anything*. And they wouldn't care.

"At least you're *alive*," his father had told him once when he was little. He had fallen down in the road and skinned his knee. He'd run to his dad for comfort, crying. His father had been disgusted with him. "Pain makes you strong," he'd said. "It means you're still alive. Your sister can't feel any pain where she is."

It was always there: Penny. Even dead, she

was still their favorite. He knew that his parents wished *he* had been the one who'd died, not Penny. He didn't really blame them. There were plenty of times when he wished exactly the same thing.

There was a howl outside in the night. A police car, heading off somewhere. His throat tightened as he saw the flash of lights zip across the ceiling. Would they stop here one of these days? Would the cops come for him?

Why did he think he really had killed Penny? Maybe, even at the age of four, he'd hated the comparisons between them. Maybe he'd thought with Penny gone his parents would love him and pay attention to him.

Well, if that had been his motive, it hadn't worked. He was less loved now than he had ever been. Dead, Penny was no longer a sweet daughter. She was a saint!

But not to him. Never to him.

That made him pause. As tired as he was, he knew he'd always had some hostile feelings toward his older sister.

At long last he fell asleep. This time the nightmare would be complete. And twisting through it were memories of Penny. The gentle smile. The long, shiny blond hair. The careful hand movements. The spotless bedroom, and . . .

The *truth*.

8

The Final Nightmare

Matt couldn't believe how much he was shaking. He swallowed nervously as he walked across the cemetery toward his sister's grave. Now he remembered it all. In the depths of the night, his memories had flooded back to him.

He knew now *who* had killed Penny.

It was a spectacular morning, not too humid or hot yet. The cemetery had never looked more peaceful, more beautiful. Two grave dig-

119

gers were finishing up a fresh grave as he walked past them. They had dug the hole already, piling the soil on a large plastic sheet, in order not to bury the neat grass of the lawns. One man rested on his shovel, giving Matt a cheery wave. Matt nodded back.

Life went on. Death went on. It was just a normal day for them. For Matt, it was a chance for peace.

She was waiting for him as he approached Penny's grave. Penny Gillis, waiting, watching, as he walked up. She was dressed in white. Her hands were clasped in front of her, holding a small white handbag. She had a faintly wistful smile on her face.

He walked toward her, his face expressionless.

"It's me, isn't it?" he asked her. "I'm the one you want."

The smile spread across her whole face now. "So you *have* remembered," she said. "I knew you would, in time."

"Oh, I remembered," he agreed. "*Everything.*"

"Good." She smiled again. "Do you want to talk about it?"

"It came back to me during the night," he told her. "Finally, it's all clear to me. That day, and everything else. . . ."

"I hate you!" he screamed. "I hate you!"

Penny sneered back at him. "Crybaby!" she jeered. "Go on, tell Mom. See who *she* believes!"

His head hurt. Penny had slapped him so hard that he couldn't think straight. But even at the age of four, Matt knew Penny was right. His parents *never* believed him when he told them about Penny. Never.

"She's our angel," Mom would say. "Such a *good* girl. So kind and thoughtful."

It wasn't true, any of it. It was just an image Penny carefully invented. When anyone was around, Penny would be gentle and considerate. When she was alone with Matt, her abuse would begin.

She was very clever about it. She never hit him hard enough to break the skin, or give him any bad bruises. But she hit him hard enough to hurt. And she constantly shoved him, pulled his hair, or hung him upside down by his ankles. She would push him to the limit, but never, ever, any further.

"Why did you spoil it all?" she'd scream at him. "Until *you* were born, I was their favorite. They didn't need you—they had *me*! And I don't need you!" She pushed her twisted face down near his smaller, scared one. "And someday, when I can get away with it, I'll get rid of you. Someday, when they won't know it was me. And when you're gone, we'll be happy again."

He tried to tell his mom and dad, but they would never listen. Penny was so sweet, they couldn't ever imagine her doing half of the things Matt accused her of doing. And he didn't have the words to explain how she was deceiving them.

Mom and Dad thought he was a sickly kid, always throwing up his food. They had no idea that Penny was constantly putting pepper in it, or worse things. Then she'd force-feed him till he was sick. If he threw up on her, she'd slam him around. When their folks came home, Penny would simply sigh angelically. "He did it again, Mom," she'd say. "I'm sorry you've got more laundry to do." And they fell for it. Every time.

He was terrified of her—and he had hated her.

The only one on Matt's side was Ralph. Ralph loved him with the unconditional love only a dog can give. Ralph was Matt's only friend, the only one who never hurt him or ignored him.

Penny, of course, hated Ralph almost as much as she hated Matt. The dog—knowing as dogs do what she was like inside—never trusted her. She was wary of Ralph. He'd never bitten her or threatened her, but he didn't care for her. He always kept one eye on Penny when they were in the same room together. One day, Ralph had come inside with a gash in his side. Matt had never been able to prove it, but he was certain Penny was responsible. *She* claimed that one of the neighborhood boys had thrown a sharp rock at Ralph. No one ever questioned her story.

Then one day it all came to a head. Mom and Dad had gone shopping, leaving the two of them and Ralph alone for a short while. Uncle Joey had promised to pop over and check in on them, to make sure everything was all right. Matt had tried to stay out of Penny's way, but it was never very easy. He'd been playing ball with Ralph. The door to the basement was slightly open, and the rubber ball had bounced down the stairs. Ralph had hurled himself after it, stomping hard on Penny's foot as he chased the ball.

"That's the last straw, you stinking animal!" she screamed. She stormed down the steps to the basement after him.

Matt was terrified. Penny was bad enough at the best of times, but when she got mad like this, anything could happen. And he couldn't let her hurt Ralph again. He had to stop her.

Standing at the top of the stairs, he stared down into the dark basement. The stairs were awfully steep. Then he heard Penny scream and kick something over. Ralph whimpered with pain. Matt *had* to be brave and go after his only friend. Clutching the rail in his small hand, he started down the stairs.

While he slowly went down step by step, he heard the sounds of Penny throwing things. Mostly they missed Ralph. She was so mad that her aim wasn't very good. She was getting

angrier and angrier, her rage building as she failed to really hurt the dog. Once in a while, Ralph would give a yelp of pain as something struck him.

The light in the basement was on, and Penny must have bumped into it. The bare bulb was swaying on the end of its cord, throwing shifting shadows all over the place. As Matt made it safely to the bottom, he stood there, trying to see what was going on.

Ralph was limping. His right front paw seemed to be hurt. Penny must really have injured him this time. Every ounce of hatred in Matt's tiny body exploded at once. "Don't hurt Ralph!" he yelled and threw himself at his sister, arms swinging wildly.

One punch hit her hard enough in the stomach to make her yell. Penny was shaking with anger now. "You stupid little brat!" she screamed, and gave him a slap that sent him spinning into the wall.

Pain exploded in him as he fell on the bare concrete. With a cry, he tried to get out of her way. Tears and sobs almost choked him.

It was too much for Ralph. With a savage snarl, he leaped at Penny.

She screamed with terror as the dog slammed into her. She fell backward, against the workbench where their dad kept all his tools. It must have hurt her, because she cried out. Ralph was on the attack now. As Penny tried to fend him off, he barked viciously and went for her throat.

Penny threw the enraged animal across the floor. Ralph whimpered with pain as his bad paw hit the floor. Then he struggled back to his feet and went at her again. All the while, Matt lay in the shadows, watching through his tears.

Penny had panicked and snatched up the first thing that came to hand—a woodworking knife. She thrust it at Ralph as he came at her with his mouth open wide, teeth bared. Ralph howled as Penny plunged the knife into his side. She stabbed him again and again, in a kind of frenzy. But the poor dog had collapsed to the floor after the first blow.

Finally she was too tired to strike again. She wiped her hair back from her face. Her hand left a streak of blood across her pale skin. She stared down at Ralph's dead body in annoyance, as if blaming him for having died. She was red with his blood, her clothing an absolute mess. There wasn't going to be any way she'd worm her way out of taking the rap for this.

Then she saw Matt. Her eyes were full of hate. She couldn't blame this on him. She'd killed Ralph and her clothes would prove it. He'd fix her for that! She saw his expression and must have understood.

"You killed Ralph!" he accused her, getting weakly to his feet. "I'm tellin' Mommy!"

"No, you aren't," she said, coldly. There was a very odd look in her eyes that scared him. "It was one of the neighborhood kids who did this. I just got bloody from trying to help Ralph."

"You did it," Matt insisted. "I saw you!"

"I didn't, you little jerk," she snapped. The knife was still in her hand, dripping Ralph's blood on the concrete floor. With a snarl, she lunged at him.

Matt fell to his knees and scrambled between her legs. Then, terror giving him the strength he needed, he ran into the shadows outside the range of the single light bulb. He slipped into a small gap under the stairs and held his breath, waiting.

"Come out, you slime," Penny growled, clutching the bloody knife. She hadn't seen where he'd hidden, but she knew the direction he'd taken. His heart pounded fiercely as she drew closer, her mad eyes darting from side to side as she looked for him.

She was going to kill him! Matt knew this with absolute certainty. She'd always hated and resented him. Now, he would be able to shatter her image as a sweet, innocent girl by telling his parents how she had killed Ralph. But Penny wouldn't let that happen. She'd rather silence him for good than be found out. She'd find someone to pin the blame on and would probably even claim she'd tried to help Matt and Ralph, but without any luck. Matt had to do something fast.

In a flood of panic, he did the only thing that he could think of—he jumped out of his hiding place and headed straight for her. He was going to do just what Ralph had tried to do— knock her down, so he could run upstairs.

Penny was looking away from his hiding

spot when he jumped up. As she turned, he rammed into her legs. Caught completely off guard, Penny lost her balance and spun around. She fell toward their dad's worktable. Penny tried to catch herself as she fell, but only her elbow hit the table. She fell awkwardly across her arm as she slipped to the floor.

Matt heard a ripping sound as Penny hit the concrete. She shuddered, and then slowly rolled onto her back. She'd fallen on the knife. It stuck straight up out of her. Penny gasped in pain and tried to sit up. Blood was suddenly everywhere. He crawled toward her. Warm stickiness seeped onto him. He screamed in terror, thinking for a second that this was another of her mean tricks.

It wasn't. The light in her eyes faded. Her body twitched and then lay perfectly still.

Horrified, Matt tried to pull the knife out of her. If he could get it out, maybe she'd wake up.

There was a noise at the basement window, and Matt looked up. He saw the horrified face of Uncle Joey staring down at him. His hands were still on the slippery handle of the knife. . . .

9

Peace at Last

Matt straightened up with a jerk. He realized he'd just told Penny the whole story. He'd become completely absorbed in his memories, now that they were clear.

"I tried to explain it," he told her. "But Mom and Dad never listened to me. They always thought that you were a saint. They never believed there was any evil in you. They thought I'd gone downstairs after you'd been killed and found you there." He shook his head. "They

131

were so sure you were an angel that I guess I buried all my memories. I was only four. My mind covered up the truth because it didn't fit with what everyone told me *must* have happened. Like the others, I started to think you were a sweet girl, too. Only, deep down, I knew it wasn't true. I hated you, but I never knew why. I thought there was something wrong with me, that it was all my fault, but it wasn't *me*—it was you."

For the first time in his life, everything was starting to make sense to Matt. "That's why I get these sudden rages," he said. "It happens whenever I'm blamed for things I haven't done. I guess I'm striking back at *you*. It's why I beat up Laney Mills that time. She'd been teasing me, just the way you always did." He stared at Penny, finally understanding. "I can see what I've been doing now, and why," he told her. "I wasn't the one who was bad—it was you."

"And you're convinced now that I really am your sister, Penny, back from the dead?" she asked him mockingly.

"Well—yeah. You look *exactly* like her."

Matt frowned at her. "But why are you back? And why are you doing this?"

Penny smiled and opened her purse. "Some of what I told you is true," she said. "Some of it I'd better explain so you'll understand." She held up the tape recorder that Uncle Joey had given her. "Uncle Joey is convinced that you killed Penny. He gave me this tape recorder to tape your 'confession.' He thinks that he and I set up this whole plan to make you crack and admit that you killed your sister."

Matt frowned. "Plan? Confession? What are you talking about?"

"He saw you that day in the basement, remember? He was certain he'd seen you kill Penny, though no one would believe him. In the end, they sent him to the funny farm. Then one day he started writing to a girl named Penny Gillis, a girl who looked *exactly* like your dead sister. After he met her and saw how much she resembled Penny Howard, he decided to use the coincidence to pay you back for the murder and for putting him away for so long. He suggested playing a mind game with you. He'd coach Penny Gillis so that she could impersonate the dead Penny Howard. Then he'd have the new Penny haunt you by saying she was your sister reincarnated. He hoped you would be so freaked out that you would confess to the murder. With a tape of that confession, he'd go to the police and have you finally arrested for murder."

The whole bottom seemed to fall out from under him. "It . . . it was all a trick?" he whispered, stunned. "You're not really Penny? You're a fake?" He shook his head, hardly able to believe it. "But . . . then . . . the trick backfired! Instead of taping a confession, you taped the *truth*—that it was Penny who killed herself!"

"I never turned the tape recorder on, you idiot," Penny hissed fiercely. "And I didn't say I was a fake—I said Uncle Joey *thought* I was a fake."

Matt's head was whirling. "But . . . why? I mean, why not turn the tape on?"

"You're pathetic. You know that?" Penny sighed. "I didn't turn the stupid thing on because I knew you weren't going to confess to the murder. And I *am* Penny Howard. *I* set this whole thing up. I just let Uncle Joey think it was his idea. He thinks it was just a coincidence that he met me. I had to work really hard to set that up! I suggested the community project to my teacher to give me an excuse to write to him. Then I prodded him into this silly plot to get you to confess. What a jerk! He thinks this was all *his* idea, but it's mine. He doesn't know that I'm Penny Howard, but you and I know better. And somehow that dumb Pueblo seemed to know, too."

Something fell into place in his mind. "So you killed Pueblo."

Penny nodded. The smile hadn't left her face. Matt knew she was still a sickie, Penny Howard or Penny Gillis. She might have changed her body, but she was just the same. She was hiding behind a beautiful face and an innocent appearance.

"But why?" he asked.

"I saw him," she replied. "He was trying to suck up to you. Just the way Ralph always had. I *hated* him, just as I hated Ralph. Both of them liked you, not me." Her eyes gleamed with an evil light. "You always tried to get everyone to like you instead of me. Mom and Dad, Ralph, and even Pueblo."

Matt shook his head, disgusted. "You're really sick. You know that? Penny Howard killed Ralph, so you killed your own dog. Wow! You're nuts."

Penny cocked her head to one side and gave him a sweet smile. "The police think *you* did it. You made my mom suspicious last night. This morning, just before I left, I told her your real name and address. I told her you'd been harassing me for some reason. That you'd been threatening me." She grinned, showing her perfect teeth. "She thinks *you* killed Pueblo as a warning to me."

"It's no good," he told her. He felt nothing but contempt for her pathetic trickery. "The police won't believe it. Why should they?"

She shook her head. "You're so *dumb*. You know that? You always were. Growing ten years older hasn't changed you one bit. You're still stupid."

"Say what you like," he replied. "It doesn't matter. Now that I know the truth about you and what happened, I'll find some way to prove it."

"No, you won't," she said. "Honestly, you're just so mega-stupid, aren't you?" She smiled again, but this time it was twisted. Her eyes held an inner fire of dangerous intensity. "I *told* you I was back for revenge. This is all a part of it. But you *had* to remember everything, or there wouldn't be enough fun in it."

"Revenge?" He gave a hollow laugh. "How can you do that? *You* killed yourself. *You're* the murderer. Who are you trying to punish?"

"*You!*" she snarled. "It was all your fault! Once you came along, everything was ruined. Till then, Mom and Dad and I had a perfect life. Then you wrecked it. And when I tried to make it right by taking you out of the picture, you ruined even that. But *this* time you won't spoil the ending."

Matt stared at her in shock. She sounded as if she'd completely flipped! She thought she really was Penny Howard. Then she opened her handbag again. This time she pulled out a knife. It was thick, with a sharp point and a heavy blade.

"My father's hunting knife," she explained. "It was stolen a couple weeks ago." She smiled, gently. "Someone broke into the house when we were all out and stole a lot of things. By now I'm sure the police will think it was you."

"Don't be silly," Matt said nervously. "Think about what you're doing."

"I *have* thought!" she yelled. "I've done nothing else *but* think about this since my memory came back. I don't want to be in the Gillis family. I was happy with Mom and Dad. It's your fault I'm back like this, and I'm going to get you for it. This time, I'm going to kill *you*!"

She really *was* crazy! Even though she knew the truth, she was twisting it in her own mind to make him look guilty—because he'd fought back! "Hey, Penny, calm down," he urged her.

"Calm?" she sneered, raising the knife. "How *can* I be calm? You've just attacked me and want to murder me. I'll manage to break free, though, and stab you in self-defense. *Then* I'll be happy. Then I'll have my revenge."

Matt knew that she meant what she was saying. She'd really set up this whole deal. And it all ended with his murder. Here—at her own grave. It was sensational. Sick, but sensational.

If she could kill him.

For a second Matt stood frozen in disbelief.

Then Penny lunged for him, and his mind began to work again. He jerked aside, and the knife narrowly missed slicing his throat. It nicked him as he moved, though, and he felt a sharp pain and a trickle of blood.

He pushed out at Penny, shoving her away from him. She stumbled back, into her own gravestone. It kept her from falling, and she clutched at it for support.

Matt wanted to try to talk her out of this, but he could see madness in her eyes. There was no way to avoid this fight. He didn't want to do it, but he wasn't really left with any choice in the matter. He was bigger than she this time, and a lot stronger. She couldn't overpower him. Now *he* was the older and stronger one.

With a burst of anger, he jumped at her. She tried to thrust the knife blade between them, to impale him on it. His arm passed below the thrust, and he jerked upward. He grabbed her wrist tightly with one hand, forcing the knife away from him. With his other hand, he grabbed a handful of her long hair, jerking her backwards.

Penny screamed and kicked at him. There

was a flash of pain as her shoe connected with his shin, but he refused to give in. Holding her wrist tightly, he slammed her hard against the gravestone. The edge of it caught the back of her hand. The knife fell to the grass, and she screamed in frustration.

She was no longer a threat. Now all he had to do was calm her down. She needed serious help—Penny Howard or Penny Gillis. If he could only reason with her. But as he looked at her face twisted in rage he somehow knew that he would never be rid of her. She was his enemy—for life.

Then, suddenly, there was another person with them. An arm snaked around Matt's neck, jerking his head back with a crack. Matt was shocked and let go of Penny. She kicked him again as she broke free. Matt was thrown off balance by the unexpected attack from behind. He started to fall forward. Something came down hard on his right arm, and he cried out. He tried to straighten up, and then he saw who had attacked him.

It was Uncle Joey.

He looked even worse than usual. His face

was unwashed and unshaven. His clothing was a mess. He carried a walking stick, which he had used to hit Matt. It was raised in the air now, as if Uncle Joey planned to hit him again.

"Don't!" cried Matt, throwing his good arm in front of his face.

"I saw you!" the old man roared. "I knew you'd do it! I saw you!"

"What are you talking about?" Matt shouted. His arm throbbed with flashes of pain. He wondered whether it was broken.

"I saw you kill your sister ten years ago," Uncle Joey snarled. His eyes bored into Matt, his face a mask of disgust. "But nobody believed me. They thought I was wrong. You were too young to have stabbed her. I must have been mistaken. But I know what I saw."

"No," Matt tried to explain. "It wasn't—"

"You needn't lie to me," the old man replied, holding his stick ready to strike again. "I know what I saw. I knew you were a killer. So I talked this young girl into helping me catch you. And now you almost killed *her*!"

"No!" Matt insisted. "You've got it wrong! I didn't—"

"Save your lying breath!" Uncle Joey told him. "I saw you trying to kill her with my own eyes. I told those grave diggers to call the police. Then I rushed over as fast as I could. I got here just in time to stop you from murdering again."

"Oh, *thank you!*" Penny said, theatrically. "I was so terrified. It was *horrible*. He kept saying all kinds of wild things. He really thinks I'm his sister and he wants to kill me again."

"Don't listen to her!" Matt cried. But he could see that there was no point. Uncle Joey was already convinced of the truth before he'd arrived here. The facts didn't matter one bit. And Matt knew that Penny would convince everyone that he was the one at fault. Even if she couldn't kill him, she could certainly get him put in jail or sent away. That might be enough revenge to make her happy.

He couldn't allow that to happen. He knew she'd twist the facts and lie with a straight face. And he had no doubt—given his record of school fights—whom the police would believe. He'd lose this one if they found him here.

He had to escape and get some time to think. Maybe he could come up with some way to prove his innocence. But he knew he'd never get a chance here and now.

Penny was playing her rescued maiden role to the hilt now. "He's a beast!" she sobbed. "He was going to kill me!"

"There, there," Uncle Joey said, uncomfortably. "You're safe now." He half turned to hold her.

This was his chance! Matt jumped to his feet and pushed the two of them together. Then he spun around and ran as fast as he could down the hill. He had to get to his bike and break all speed records to escape. He didn't know what he was going to do, but he'd work it out. He just had to get free.

There was another cry from behind. Uncle Joey was on his feet. He waved his stick and set off after Matt. For an old man, he seemed to have a lot of energy. Penny, much younger and faster, was already only twenty feet or so behind him.

Heart pounding, arms pumping, he dashed down the pathway toward the main gate. His vision was blurry, and the arm that had been hit hurt like crazy. He hoped he'd be able to get away.

Straining his ears, he heard Penny running and breathing hard behind him. As he dashed across the bottom of the hill for the gates, he heard the far-off *whoop, whoop* of a police siren.

They were here! He was going to get caught!

Straining to get every last bit of energy into his legs, Matt shot toward the cemetery gate.

He looked over his shoulder as his foot hit the entrance road. Penny had stopped. She was standing dead still behind him, smiling.

Then he heard the car.

He turned his head toward the sound. He saw everything with a strange, crystal clearness.

A hearse had just come through the cemetery gates. One of the grave diggers began to shout. But the huge, shiny, black thing was directly in front of him. He heard the tires, the horn, the squealing brakes.

Hopelessly, he threw his arms in front of his

face as the immense hearse slammed into him.

He was killed instantly.

The policeman closed his notebook with a snap and slid it back into his pocket. Penny looked up at him with real tears in her eyes. He mistook them for tears of shock and terror.

"Don't think about it," the cop said to her kindly. "It was a horrible accident, I know. But it's over." He glanced to one side, where the ambulance men were loading Matt's body into the back of their vehicle. There was just a bit of blood on the road where he had landed.

Penny raged inside. *It wasn't fair!* She had wanted to kill Matt herself! And, instead, he'd been hit by the jerky driver of a stupid hearse! Tears of anger trickled down her face.

The funeral had come to a shocked halt when the hearse hit Matt. For a moment, the people in the funeral party were too stunned to continue. They wandered around aimlessly, not quite sure of what to do next.

Uncle Joey was being helpful again. The old

idiot really believed every word she'd said. He was giving a statement to the police that was bound to put her completely in the clear. Matt's death would be ruled an accident—and everyone would say how lucky she was not to have gotten hurt when he attacked her.

Well, at least Matt *was* dead. And, even if it was indirectly, she *had* killed him. That felt good. She supposed she had gotten her revenge. The thought cheered her a little.

"Do you want to go to the hospital, miss?" the policeman asked her.

"What?" she looked at him, puzzled.

"Just a checkup," he told her. "You've been through a lot here. It must have been a terrible shock when the boy attacked you."

"Oh. No, I'll be okay, I think." Penny smiled winningly at Uncle Joey. "If it hadn't been for this dear man here, I'd probably be dead by now."

Uncle Joey smiled at the praise. "I'm just glad I was in time," he said, modestly. "He was off his rocker—trying to kill again, and right over his sister's grave, too."

What an old fool! Still, he would be her cover

forever. Nobody would dream of suggesting any other possible explanation for what had happened here. Penny felt better for that. Matt was dead, she was vindicated, and that was what mattered, after all.

She'd gotten away with murder. Literally.

When the policeman insisted on helping her in some way, Penny allowed him to take her home. All the way back, she kept replaying the memory of the hearse slamming into Matt and killing him. She felt good, she decided. She'd won.

As they pulled up outside her house, an old lady hurried over to them. It was that nosy old Mrs. Brennan from across the street. Penny smiled sweetly at her. "Hi, Mrs. Brennan! It's all right. Don't worry."

"I'm so glad the police found you," the old woman said. "I was waiting for you to come home so I could tell you."

"Tell me what?" Penny struggled to stay polite.

"It's your mother. She had to be rushed to the hospital."

"What?" Penny shouted. She'd been expecting to be able to trade off her "terrible ordeal" for some special attention over the next couple of weeks at least! Now her mother was in the hospital?

"She's okay," Mrs. Brennan answered her. "She was in labor." Seeing Penny's blank look, she explained: "She's having her *baby!*"

Epilogue

There was peace at last. Matt was warm and comfortable, gently floating in nothingness. It felt good and quiet here. The fuzziness was making him very drowsy. It was really hard to think. But he felt completely at ease. All he could hear was the sound of a heart beating. Such a warm and comforting sound.

This was what he'd always wanted. No problems. No cares. Nothing. Just peace. Maybe he should be grateful for . . .

For what? He couldn't quite recall. There had been *something* before this wonderful peace, but he couldn't quite remember what it had been.

Something about a sister . . . Yes, that was it. Something to do with a sister. Penny . . . Penny, that was the name! There was something she'd done, and something yet to be done.

Oh, well. Right now, he just wanted to enjoy this calm, peaceful sensation. . . . He was *so* relaxed.

Then, suddenly, it stopped. There was a feeling of great pressure. Now his whole world was exploding!

"There we are, Mrs. Gillis." The nurse—a cheery woman with laughing eyes—passed over the warmly wrapped baby. "It's a boy."

"A boy . . ." Mrs. Gillis smiled weakly. She hugged the tiny bundle to herself in weary happiness. "Oh, but he looks so serious." She looked down at the tiny face. The baby's eyes seemed focused and intense.

"Don't worry," the nurse replied. "They all look that way now and then. It's not as comfy out here in the real world, I suppose." She smiled down at the mother and child. "He's a pretty little thing, you know. Do you have a name for him yet?"

"Oh, yes," Mrs. Gillis said, hugging her new child. "We're going to call him Matthew—Matt for short."

DON'T MISS
THESE
SHOCKING
STORIES...

NIGHT WINGS

A nightmare car accident changes Rob Jensen's life forever. In one night he is transformed from a high school jock to a freakish medical guinea pig. He wants to escape. In desperation he accepts a mysterious job offer in Romania. A job so horrifying it tests the very limits of Rob's sanity. But is the work too dangerous for Rob — or is Rob too dangerous for the work?

BLOOD
WOLF

Numin, the second son of the murdered King Kardak, is very popular with the people of Mestain. This angers his evil brother, Duroc. Young Numin must flee Mestain to escape the assassins hired by his brother. But dark prophesies and mysterious dreams indicate a violent death for Numin. And the wolves…what about the wolves…. Is there something more terrifying than his deepest fears?

ALIEN PREY

Life is pretty dull in Baine's Hollow for Josh and his wild buddies, Paul, Beth, and Ben. But when a stranger comes to town, people begin to die…in horrible ways. And the funny thing is, no one seems to care. What's going on? Who's in charge here? The town has a secret—a terrible secret—and dying is just the beginning.